"You don't want to be labeled a culinary tease now, do you?" Stone asked the question so seriously, for a moment Danni didn't realize that he was kidding her.

"Heaven forbid!" She laughed. He was being kind, and she appreciated it.

"Good, then go whip up something. Impress me with your ability to create something delicious out of nothing."

"I'll do my best." It felt good to laugh, she thought. Good to feel useful again. A surge of deep gratitude spiked through her. "You're a good man, Stone Scarborough."

He shrugged off the compliment, not comfortable with its weight. "I'm only as good as I have to be," he told her.

Why that sounded like a promise of things to come to her she didn't know, but it did.

And it sent a little thrill of anticipation through her.

Dear Reader,

Here we are again, back in the world of the Matchmaking Mamas. This time around, Maizie Sommers, the Realtor who originally came up with the concept of finding a match for her daughter and the daughters of her friends, encounters a unique client: Ginny Scarborough. Ginny comes into her office and requests that Maizie find someone for her widower dad. Nothing unusual about that—except that Ginny is four, almost five years old, and *very* precocious. Since Ginny's dad is a general contractor and Maizie has recently sold a fixer-upper to a newly transplanted young woman who can make taste buds sit up and beg, it takes very little to bring the two together. And with Ginny as their own personal rooting section, how can anything go wrong? Want to find out? Then come, read. Enjoy!

As ever, I thank you for reading, and from the bottom of my heart I wish you someone to love who loves you back.

With affection,

Marie Ferrarella

WISH UPON A MATCHMAKER

MARIE FERRARELLA

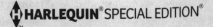

HARLEQUIN® SPECIAL EDITION®

Recycling programs
for this product may
not exist in your area.

ISBN-13: 978-0-373-65746-9

WISH UPON A MATCHMAKER

Copyright © 2013 by Marie Rydzynski-Ferrarella

H HARLEQUIN®
™ www.Harlequin.com

Printed in U.S.A.

Books by Marie Ferrarella

Harlequin Special Edition

¶A Match for the Doctor #2117
¶What the Single Dad Wants... #2122
**The Baby Wore a Badge #2131
¶¶Fortune's Valentine Bride #2167
¶Once Upon a Matchmaker #2192
§§Real Vintage Maverick #2210
¶A Perfectly Imperfect Match #2240
~~A Small Fortune #2246
¶Ten Years Later... #2252
¶Wish Upon a Matchmaker #2264

Silhouette Special Edition

~Diamond in the Rough #1910
~The Bride with No Name #1917
~Mistletoe and Miracles #1941
††Plain Jane and the Playboy #1946
~Travis's Appeal #1958
Loving the Right Brother #1977
The 39-Year-Old Virgin #1983
~A Lawman for Christmas #2006
□□Prescription for Romance #2017
¶Doctoring the Single Dad #2031
¶Fixed Up with Mr. Right? #2041
¶Finding Happily-Ever-After #2060
¶Unwrapping the Playboy #2084
°Fortune's Just Desserts #2107

Harlequin Romantic Suspense

Private Justice #1664
†The Doctor's Guardian #1675
*A Cavanaugh Christmas #1683
Special Agent's Perfect Cover #1688
*Cavanaugh's Bodyguard #1699
*Cavanaugh Rules #1715
*Cavanaugh's Surrender #1725
Colton Showdown #1732
A Widow's Guilty Secret #1736
Cavanaugh on Duty #1751

Silhouette Romantic Suspense

†A Doctor's Secret #1503
†Secret Agent Affair #1511
*Protecting His Witness #1515
Colton's Secret Service #1528

The Heiress's 2-Week Affair #1556
*Cavanaugh Pride #1571
*Becoming a Cavanaugh #1575
The Agent's Secret Baby #1580
*The Cavanaugh Code #1587
*In Bed with the Badge #1596
*Cavanaugh Judgment #1612
Colton by Marriage #1616
*Cavanaugh Reunion #1623
†In His Protective Custody #1644

Harlequin American Romance

Pocketful of Rainbows #145
°°The Sheriff's Christmas
Surprise #1329
°°Ramona and the Renegade #1338
°°The Doctor's Forever Family #1346
Montana Sheriff #1369
Holiday in a Stetson #1378
"The Sheriff Who Found Christmas"
°°Lassoing the Deputy #1402
°°A Baby on the Ranch #1410
°°Forever Christmas #1426

*Cavanaugh Justice
†The Doctors Pulaski
~Kate's Boys
††The Fortunes of Texas:
Return to Red Rock
□□The Baby Chase
¶Matchmaking Mamas
°The Fortunes of Texas:
Lost...and Found
°°Forever, Texas
**Montana Mavericks:
The Texans Are Coming!
¶¶The Fortunes of Texas:
Whirlwind Romance
§§Montana Mavericks:
Back in the Saddle
~~The Fortunes of Texas:
Southern Invasion

Other titles by this author
available in ebook format.

MARIE FERRARELLA

This *USA TODAY* bestselling and RITA® Award-winning author has written more than two hundred books for Harlequin, some under the name Marie Nicole. Her romances are beloved by fans worldwide. Visit her website, www.marieferrarella.com.

To
Andrew Gallagher,
who mentioned
his daughter's name
to me and
inspired a story.

Prologue

"**A**re you the lady who finds mommies?"

The high-pitched, rather intelligent little voice cut a hole in Maizie Sommers's mental haze. For the last half hour, the successful Realtor had been busy putting together an ad for her newest local real estate listing so that it could be entered on her website. Finding just the right words to place the proper emphasis on the twenty-year-old ranch house's best features had been nothing short of a challenge. The term *fixer-upper* carried such a negative connotation.

Absorbed in the task, Maizie had only vaguely heard the front door to her office opening and closing. It had registered as just so much background noise. Part of her thought she'd only imagined it.

Especially when she'd glanced in the direction of the door and hadn't seen anyone come in.

But there obviously was a reason for that. The person who had come in was only approximately half the size of an adult.

Maizie stopped working and after looking around, she half rose in her seat and looked over the edge of her desk. Ten small fingertips were firmly pressed against it. The little girl pushed herself up as far as she could go, standing on the very tiptoes of her black patent-leather shoes.

Maizie put down her pen and smiled at the child, judging her to be around four, or possibly a small five. Slight and a strawberry-blonde, her newest visitor had exceptionally intelligent-looking blue eyes. She was going to be a knockout in a dozen years, Maizie judged.

"Hello."

The girl, who more than anything resembled a perfect little doll, tossed her head—sending her curls bouncing—and paused only a moment to politely return the greeting, "Hello," before she got back down to business.

No doubt, she was a woman on a mission.

"Are you the lady who finds mommies?" the pint-size strawberry-blonde asked again. "My friend Greg said you found one for his dad and that she's really nice and now they're all very happy."

Maizie never forgot a name, especially not a child's name. The little girl was talking about Greg and Gary Muldare. After Sheila, Micah Muldare's aunt, had come to see her, lamenting the young widower's state, she and her two dearest friends had strategized and gotten the boys' father, Micah, together with a bright, up-and-coming dynamo of a lawyer, Tracy Ryan, who solved

Micah's legal problems and along the way wound up becoming Mrs. Micah Muldare.

Word was getting around faster and faster, Maizie mused with a smile. She'd had walk-in clients before—both for her professional services and for her unofficial ones, but none of her clients had ever come in the economy size.

"What happened to your mommy, dear?" Maizie asked the girl kindly.

And just what was the child doing here by herself? Had the little girl run away in order to come see her? Her own daughter had been precocious, but even *she* hadn't been this independent at such a young age.

There was just the slightest hint of sorrow in her voice as the girl said, "Mommy died before I could remember her, but Daddy remembers, and it makes him sad when he does. I want Daddy to be happy like Greg's daddy is." Her voice took on conviction as she said, "My daddy needs one. He needs a mommy," she clarified in case that had gotten lost in the shuffle of words. "Can you find him one? And make her pretty, because my daddy said he wants one as pretty as me. That's why he's with Elizabeth now," she confided. "She's pretty, but she's not a mommy, just a lady." Lowering her voice as she raised herself up as far as she could on her toes so that only Maizie could hear, she said in what amounted to a stage whisper, "I don't think she likes kids."

Before Maizie could recover or comment on either the little girl's request, or her summation of her father's current relationship, the door to her widely sought-after real estate agency opened a second time in the space of less than five minutes.

It wasn't that Maizie was unaccustomed to a lot of foot traffic, thanks to both her reputation and the popular shopping center location of her agency, she was more than used to a constant flow of humanity. However, the two people who worked for her were currently out showing properties, and she had no appointments on her calendar for at least an hour. She'd been promising herself a quick lunch now for the last ninety minutes—the second she finished writing the ad.

But something far more interesting had come up and her neglected stomach was pushed into second place.

Humor curved the corners of Maizie's mouth. She'd never had a walk-in who wasn't able to see over her desk before.

But just as Maizie had gotten her newest would-be client to tell her story, an utterly frazzled-looking woman suddenly burst into her real estate office. The second she did, the woman made a beeline for the tiny visitor who was standing on the other side of Maizie's desk.

"Virginia Ann Scarborough, are you trying to give me a heart attack?" the blonde demanded as she fell to her knees and smothered the little girl in a huge hug that utterly reeked of relief as well as panic.

"No," the little girl replied in a small, somewhat contrite voice. Her pained expression told Maizie that the girl was merely enduring the hug. Apparently, unlike the distraught woman who'd found her, she hadn't been at all afraid.

"I was trying to find a mommy for Daddy," the child

explained, as if that would clear everything up and ex-
onerate her as well.

"You know you're not supposed to run off like that,
Ginny," the woman chided.

Making a swift survey of the little girl, the woman
appeared satisfied that the only thing worse for wear
were her own nerves. She rose to her feet and only then
turned her attention to the other person in the room.

"I'm very sorry about this," she apologized to Maizie.
"I hope my niece didn't break anything."

"I wasn't in here long enough to break anything, Aunt
Virginia," the girl protested indignantly.

Maizie rose from behind her desk, a little bemused.
"Are you her guardian?" she asked the woman, nodding
at the little girl.

"I'm her aunt." She slanted an exasperated look at the
little girl that was nonetheless laced with love. "Her long-
suffering aunt. I swear, Ginny, if you weren't named
after me…" Ginny's aunt let her voice trail off, then
flashed another apologetic smile at Maizie as she took
a firm hold of Ginny's hand, her intent clear. She was
taking the little girl out of the office. "I'm sorry about
all this—"

"No, please, wait," Maizie coaxed in her best mater-
nal, nurturing voice. "You look a little frazzled. Let me
get you a nice cup of tea." She glanced down at Ginny.
"And I think I might have some lemonade for you if
you like."

"Yes, please," Ginny said with restrained enthusiasm.

"No, really, we've been enough trouble already," Virginia protested.

"Nonsense. You're no trouble at all and I must say my curiosity has been piqued," Maizie admitted as she went to the small island against the wall that housed an all-in-one unit, combining a small refrigerator, a stove with microwave features and a sink on one side. With a minimum of movements, she made a hot Chai tea for Virginia and poured a glass of lemonade for the small whirling dervish who'd been named after her.

"Now then, Ginny," Maizie began, addressing Ginny as she handed her the glass of lemonade, "you said something about your daddy needing a wife."

Hearing that, Virginia's eyes widened in stunned amazement. "Ginny, you didn't—why would you do that?" the woman demanded of her niece.

"Because she finds them," Ginny told her aunt, nodding at Maizie. "Greg said so," she said with the conviction of the very young.

"This lady runs a real estate agency," Virginia pointed out, her nerves beginning to fray no doubt.

"Perhaps I should explain," Maizie interjected, coming to Ginny's rescue. "My friends and I dabble in matchmaking on the side—there's no charge," she said quickly in case the other woman thought this was some sort of a scam, "just the satisfaction of bringing together two people who were meant for each other but who might never—without the proper intervention— come together," she said. Her eyes shifted to Ginny. "Like your friend Greg's father and Tracy Ryan. My friends and I supply the 'intervention,' so to speak," she told Virginia.

"Is that why you begged me to bring you here, to the ice cream parlor?" she asked her niece.

"They have very good ice cream," Ginny piped up innocently.

"See what I'm up against?" Virginia asked Maizie wearily.

Maizie did her best to appear sympathetic. In her line of work, she'd had a great deal of practice. "Are you her father's sister?" she asked.

Virginia nodded. "His name is Stone Scarborough. I'm his younger sister. I moved in with him to help out after Eva—Ginny's mother—died. That was a year and a half ago. I'm still helping," she added.

And you want to move on with your life, Maizie surmised from the other woman's choice of words and her tone.

Maizie sat back in her chair, her mouth curving in a smile of anticipation. She could sense the thrill of a challenge taking hold. Nothing she loved more than being challenged.

"So, tell me about your brother," she coaxed Virginia.

"I don't know where to start," Virginia said with a sigh.

"At the beginning is always a good place," Maizie encouraged.

"I guess it is." Taking a deep breath, the other woman began to talk, with frequent interjections coming from Ginny.

Maizie listened attentively to both.

And a plan began to form.

Chapter One

Stone Scarborough stared at his younger sister, trying to make sense out of what she had, rather breathlessly, just told him.

Whatever it was, Virginia seemed very animated about it and he'd managed to glean that it had something to do with the business card she had just pressed into his hand. But her narrative came out so disjointed he found himself feeling the way he had back in the days when he'd walk into the middle of a movie with his late wife—Eva never managed to be on time for anything no matter how hard she tried—and he was forced to try to make heads or tails out of what he was subsequently watching.

In addition to Virginia's overwhelming flow of words, his daughter, Ginny, seemed to have caught the fever and was fairly bouncing up and down right in front of him. It was as if both were experiencing a massive sugar attack.

In an attempt to sort out the verbiage, Stone held his hand up to get Virginia to stop talking for a moment, regroup and begin at the beginning.

"Run this by me one more time," Stone urged his sister. "From the top," he added.

His sister Virginia shook her head, her light blond ponytail swishing from side to side. "You know, for a brilliant man, you can be so slow sometimes."

"Must be in comparison to the company I keep," he said drolly. If he practiced for a year, he'd never be able to talk as fast as his sister—or his daughter. "Humor me," he instructed, looking down at the card in his hand. "Why am I calling this woman?"

Taking a breath, Virginia recited the facts. "The number belongs to Maizie Sommers. She's a Realtor who owns her own company. She said she needs the name of a good general contractor to recommend to her clients."

He had never believed in coincidences or good fortune without there being strings of some sort, no matter how invisible, attached.

Consequently, Stone regarded the card in his hand with more than a smattering of suspicion. "And she just walked up to you and said, 'Hmm, you look like you probably know a good general contractor,' as she handed her card to you?"

"No."

Virginia closed her eyes, doing her best to get herself under control. She knew she'd gotten too excited, but the picture that Maizie Sommers had painted for her earlier today had filled her with hope. It had been a very long time since she'd seen her brother with more than an obligatory smile on his lips.

And, like her niece, she really didn't care for the woman he was currently seeing. Try as she might, she couldn't get herself to warm up to Elizabeth Wells—and she definitely didn't see the woman as being Ginny's stepmother. For one thing, the woman was not the patient sort.

"Okay, from the top," Virginia announced. "And this time," she told her brother, "try to pay attention, all right?"

"Yes, ma'am," Stone replied, executing a mock salute and doing his best to be patient.

Stone had just been on the receiving end of disappointing news. The owners of a house he was scheduled to begin work on had just changed their minds and canceled the project on him. That didn't exactly put him in the best of moods.

He didn't have time to waste like this. There were cages he needed to rattle in order to replace the work he'd lost. But Virginia had gotten right in his face and insisted that he listen to her.

"Well?" Stone prodded.

Virginia took a deep breath. She decided that she would stay as close to the truth as possible without coming right out and telling her brother that he was being set up—not to take a fall, but to fall in love. If he even *suspected* that, he would never agree to any of this. And he needed to agree because, at the very least, he would wind up earning some money doing what he did best these days—working with his hands.

Five years ago, he'd been an aerospace engineer. But that industry was all but dead in Southern California, so he had fallen back on what he'd done while working his way through college. He'd worked in construction.

But now *that* was on shaky grounds. The economy had taken a bite out of everyone's livelihood and his line of work was seeing a definite downturn. Remodeling was a luxury people felt they could put off until later without any major consequences. Virginia was confident that her brother wouldn't turn down work.

She just had to sell him on how this had all come about.

"Okay, from the top," Virginia said, echoing his words, then started with her narrative. "I took Ginny out for some ice cream."

Stone looked a wee bit exasperated. "Just what she needs, more sugar." He loved his daughter more than life itself, but there were times when getting her to behave was a challenge—one that wore him out. Stone slanted a glance toward his only child. Ginny had been in constant motion since she and Virginia had walked in. "Is that why she's bouncing five inches off the ground?" he asked.

"You're interrupting," Virginia accused, frowning at him.

He suppressed a sigh and waved his sister on. "Sorry, continue."

"Anyway, we went to that old-fashioned ice cream parlor at the Brubaker Mall, and I got her an ice cream cone. They had so many wonderful flavors to choose from, I couldn't resist so I decided that I'd get one, too—it's been a while since I just indulged in a treat," she explained by way of a sidebar.

"The point, Virginia, Get to the point," Stone directed. Ever since they were children, the shortest distance between two points for Virginia had never *once* been a straight line; it always wound up being an elaborate journey—a very pronounced squiggly line if he didn't adamantly put his foot down about it.

"Okay. While I was getting myself a cone, Ginny decided to go exploring—" Catching her lower lip between her teeth, Virginia slanted a side glance in her brother's direction. She was waiting to get the inevitable explosion out of the way.

Stone was looking sharply at his daughter. "Ginny, you know better than to go running off like that."

Rather than protest, Ginny surprised him by looking down contritely at her shoes and murmuring, "Yes, Daddy."

It wasn't that his only child was willful. She was just extremely exuberant and given to incredibly energetic enthusiasm. This apparent remorse, however, was a whole different side of her he'd never seen before.

Had something put the fear of consequences into his little girl?

Concerned, Stone glanced back at his sister for a further explanation.

Virginia instantly obliged. "I caught up with Ginny just next door. She'd wandered into a real estate office," she told him.

Stone could only stare at his sister. Ginny in a toy store he could understand, but what could have possibly attracted his precocious child to walk into a real estate office?

"Why?" he asked, looking from Ginny to his sister and then back again, waiting for one of them to give him a satisfactory answer.

Virginia was at a loss as to how to explain this part and was about to say she had no idea why Ginny did half the things she did when Ginny suddenly said, "I heard you say that you didn't know if you could find enough work to pay the bills, so I asked the lady if any of the houses in the pictures needed fixing—'cause you could do it."

Virginia was as stunned as her brother with her niece's creative explanation. It took her a beat to pick up the lifeline that had just been thrown her way.

"As it turned out, she did," Virginia confirmed belatedly. "Your daughter charmed her," Virginia said, putting her arm around Ginny's small shoulders, "and instead of just ushering us out, the woman said that as a matter of fact, she was currently looking for a good general contractor for her reference file. Naturally, Ginny and I told her you were the best, so she gave me her card and said that you should call her when you had the time."

It sounded like a fairy tale, but in there somewhere Stone assumed was the truth, otherwise, why had the woman given his sister her card? And, since he suddenly found himself unexpectedly free, what did he have to lose by calling?

"Well," Stone said slowly, looking the card over again,

"I could always use another contact but…" He glanced at his daughter, concerned and reading his own interpretation into what she'd just said. "Honey, we're going to be just fine," he assured her. "I don't want you worrying about things like bills for a long time to come. I'll take care of us," he promised.

"Yes, Daddy." Ginny smiled at him. It was the same smile he'd seen on her mother's face, Stone thought with a pang. A smile he missed seeing. "I just wanted to help," she told him.

"You do, honey, just by being you, you do," Stone assured her. He regarded the card again. No time like the present, he decided. "Okay, let's see what this Maizie Sommers has to say."

Ginny crossed her index finger and middle finger on both hands and held them up for him to see as he took out his cell phone.

We've got a great little girl, Eva. God but I wish you were here to see her, Stone couldn't help thinking as he called the number on the card.

He had no way of knowing that his daughter wasn't crossing her fingers because she was hoping he'd wind up with a job. Ginny was hoping that the "nice lady at the agency" would do for her father what she'd already done for Greg's father and that was to find her father someone who would be her new mommy.

Stone returned his daughter's hopeful smile as he heard the phone ringing on the other end.

It rang a total of two times and then he could hear the other end pick up. A sunny voice was saying, "This is Maizie Sommers, how can I help you?"

Stone turned away from his daughter and his sister, focusing his attention on the person on the other end of the call.

"Ms. Sommers, this is Stone Scarborough—" He got no further than that.

"Ah, yes," Maizie said warmly, "the general contractor. I've been waiting for your call."

Her admission caught him off guard. "You have?" Was business on her end bad, too? And if so, then what sort of work could she possibly have for him? Still, he'd called so he might as well see where this actually wound up leading.

"Absolutely," she replied. "Are you by any chance available tonight?"

"Tonight?" he echoed, wondering if he'd just made a big mistake.

Something didn't seem right. Maybe this woman wasn't looking for a general contractor but for something else entirely. Granted this Maizie Sommers didn't sound as eager and excited as Virginia had when she'd told him about this, but the woman was incredibly cheerful. Too cheerful to be talking strictly about work.

Several possibilities ran through his head, but he tamped them down until he had more to go on. No point in thinking the worst—yet.

"Yes. Or if that's too short a notice for you, then perhaps tomorrow evening might be better for you."

She kept specifying evenings, which made it sound way too much like making arrangements for a date. "Why not in the daytime?" he asked suspiciously.

The woman took the question in stride, making it

sound as if she was already prepared for it. Maybe he was being too suspicious, Stone told himself.

"I'm afraid the woman I'm giving your name to isn't available during the daytime," Maizie told him. "At least, not until the weekend. She's busy taping her program during the day," Maizie explained.

"Her program?" Stone repeated, confused.

This was a lot like talking to Virginia, he thought, wondering if vague obscurity was a gender thing or if he was just slow, the way Virginia had accused him of being. Either way, he was in need of either a further explanation—or subtitles.

"Yes, she has a daily cooking show broadcast on a cable network and right now, her weekdays are taken up taping the program before a studio audience. When she first came out here and signed her contract," Maizie continued proudly, "I sold her this lovely house. That was about six months ago.

"I got her a really good deal on the house, but that was because the owner was in a hurry to sell. The house needed a lot of work and it was sold as is. She didn't have the time then, or, I suspect, the money, for repairs. The poor dear was just starting out. But the program's doing really well and she feels that she can finally afford to have the house fixed up the way she'd like." Maizie paused for a moment, letting that all sink in before she asked him, "Are you interested, Mr. Scarborough?"

It was work. He was *more* than interested. "Yes, of course I am." But he had a question of his own. "Don't you want to see some of my work before you refer me to someone?"

She liked the fact that he was cautious and that he wasn't trying to rush her into any sort of an agreement. For her part, she had already researched his background and had seen all she needed to. Virginia Scarborough had shown her a photograph of her brother and given her enough background information to get her started in the right direction.

She felt she had the perfect match for Ginny's father. Matches usually didn't present themselves *this* quickly. They ordinarily took a little time. However, this time she'd thought of Danni almost immediately.

That, to her, was a very good sign.

"Your sister and daughter speak quite highly of you, Mr. Scarborough."

"And that's enough?" he asked rather skeptically.

"Yes," Maizie told him with feeling, and then added with a slight chuckle, "of course, what I saw on your webpage didn't exactly hurt, either."

"My webpage?" Stone echoed, confused. He turned to look quizzically at his sister as he said it. This was all news to him.

"Yes, your sister very kindly gave me the URL address. I must say it was very impressive, Mr. Scarborough," Maizie said warmly. "If my house was in need of work, I would hire you in a minute."

He supposed that was good news, but he was still a little confused. "Thanks," he murmured belatedly.

Poor man was probably still trying to figure out what hit him, Maizie thought, amused.

"So, do I have your permission to pass your name on to my client?" she asked. Maizie had learned that it never paid to appear to take things for granted. People liked the illusion of being in charge of their own fate—even when they weren't.

"Yes, of course," Stone said with feeling. If this was on the level—and it was beginning to sound that way—he definitely wanted the work. He made a point of never turning anything down.

"Wonderful," Maizie said, enthused. "I'm sure you'll be hearing from her shortly," she promised. "Just so you know, her name is Danni Everett."

"Danni Everett," he repeated.

Despite what the woman on the other end of the line had said about a cooking program on one of the cable channels, the name was not familiar to him. But then, he didn't exactly spend his days watching cable channels or any other channels for that matter. When he wasn't working—or trying to land work—he spent time with Ginny. That meant being outdoors, not locked in some room with the TV on, tuned to some brain-crushing program.

Stone politely ended the call and then turned to look at his sister again.

"My webpage?" he asked. "I thought we were going to discuss that." The last he remembered, he'd told Virginia he'd get back to her. She'd obviously decided to go on without him.

"We did discuss it," Virginia told him innocently. "You said we'd talk about it when you had time. I decided that would take too long so I just put a few simple things together. You can change it any way you want."

"Oh, thanks," he said sarcastically.

Virginia sighed. Stone had to be dragged, kicking and

screaming, into the present century for his own good. "Look, I do your accounting for you. I've got access to all your old jobs and the before-and-after photos you always take."

Photos, he thought, that his sister had insisted he take before and after undertaking each job that came his way in order to keep an accurate record of the work that he did do. He was a detail man only insofar as the actual construction work that he did. The other details, organizing the before-and-after photographs, keeping them readily accessible, well, he wasn't so good at that. But luckily, he now had to admit, Virginia was.

And apparently, she'd put that talent to work. But Stone didn't want her thinking she was off the hook just yet.

"Just how long has this webpage been up?" he asked.

"About a week," Virginia answered. However, she avoided looking at him when she said it.

"No, it's longer than that, Aunt Virginia," Ginny piped up. "You told Maizie it was up for two months."

Virginia offered her brother a forced smile. "I exaggerated," she told him.

"To whom?" he asked. "Her or me?"

"Um…"

The time didn't matter as much as the actual deed. "The point is, Virginia, you put up the webpage without telling me."

"I was waiting for the right time to tell you," she answered. It looked as if she had waited too long. With a sigh of surrender, she said, "I guess this is it."

Virginia took her netbook out of her purse, turned it

on and then typed in the appropriate address. Once the website was up, she turned the computer around so that the screen faced him.

"What do you think?"

Stone took in the various photographs he'd taken of his work, work he was very proud of and with good reason. Still, he shrugged carelessly. "Not bad."

That sounded like typical Stone, Virginia thought. He wasn't exactly heavy-handed with his praise. Nonetheless, she splayed a hand over her chest, tilting her head back dramatically as she cried, "Oh, be still my heart. I don't know if I can handle such heady praise."

Stone got the message. And, in all honesty, the website did look rather impressive. She'd done a commendable job.

"Okay, good." He paused. "Better than good," he amended.

Virginia did a rapid movement with her hand, urging him on. "Keep going," she coaxed.

The phone rang just then. "Later," he told his sister. Taking his cell out again, he answered the call. "Hello?"

"Is this Scarborough Construction?" an exceedingly melodic voice on the other end of the call asked.

He thought he detected just a trace of a Southern accent in the woman's voice. He caught himself trying to place it.

"Yes," he replied, wondering if this was the woman the Realtor had just told him about. Could she have gotten back to them so quickly?

He was all set to doubt it, but then he heard the woman with the melodic voice say, "Maizie Sommers gave me your phone number. I was wondering if we could get together tomorrow evening…if you're free, that is. I'd like to show you around my home and explain to you what I'd like to have done."

He felt as if he were standing in the direct path of a city-owned snowplow. "Sure. What time?"

"Any time after four would be fine."

"Four-thirty?" he suggested.

"Perfect." She rattled off her address, then said, "I'll see you then."

"Four-thirty," he repeated, confirming the time just before he hung up. Turning around, he saw both his sister and his daughter smiling at him. Widely. "What?" he asked uncertainly.

"Nothing," Virginia replied quickly.

But she knew if she didn't say something, he might grow suspicious. Her brother was the type who, upon finding a pot of gold at the end of the rainbow would look around to see if there was a group of leprechauns somewhere, having fun at his expense.

"I can just hear the sound of bills getting paid," she answered cheerfully.

"Well, don't count your checks before they're written," he cautioned, thinking of the job that had just fallen through earlier. "You never know how these things can turn out."

"Sorry," Virginia murmured. "Don't know what came over me." There was a time, Virginia couldn't help remembering, when her brother was just as optimistic as she was. She missed those times.

I hope you're as good as Ginny thinks you are, Mai-

zie Sommers, Virginia said silently. *I can't wait for my brother to fall in love again and become human, like he was with Eva.*

Chapter Two

Sometimes, when Danielle Everett thought about it, it *still* took her breath away.

Three years ago, she was living in Atlanta, struggling to pay off not just her student loans but also the mountain of medical bills her father had left in his wake. At the time, she was working at an insurance company, living on a shoestring and feeling her soul being sucked away, bit by bit, with every passing day.

Back then, Danni was vainly trying to keep her head above water and wondering if her utterly unfounded optimism would eventually erode because from any angle she looked at it, her optimism had absolutely nothing to hook on to.

All she wanted back then was to wake up in the morning and not feel as if she were struggling against an oppressive feeling. She didn't want to feel that if she ever let her guard down, she'd be a victim of the dark, bottomless depression whispering along the perimeter of her very being.

Back then she'd never dreamed that she could actually wake up grinning from ear to ear—the way she did these days.

Granted she was as exhausted now as she had been back then, but then the exhaustion had come from trying to keep her footing on the treadmill she was running on—the treadmill that threatened, at any moment, to pull her under. Now she was exhausted from trying to do ten things at once. The difference being was that these were ten things she *loved* doing.

Back then she'd been a company drone, an anonymous, tiny cog in a huge machine, expected to perform and make no waves. These days she was her own person. And, in many ways, her own boss as well. She took suggestions, not orders. Which made a world of difference to her everyday existence.

And all because of a skill, a talent she'd never even thought twice about.

Danni cooked like a dream and baked like a celestial being.

It all started innocently enough. She began by cooking for friends, then for friends of friends. Friends of friends who insisted on paying her for her time and skill. Before Danni knew it, she had branched out to catering full-time. There was no room left to squeeze in her day job.

The happiest day of her life was the day Danni handed in her resignation to Roosevelt Life Insurance's actuarial department. Her second-happiest day was the day she paid off the last of her late father's medical bills. Her last student loan payment followed a year later.

She was finally solvent and didn't owe anyone anything!

By then Danni realized that she was doing far more baking than cooking. A few heady connections later and she found herself being courted to star in a brand-new cooking show.

Initially, Danni had some serious doubts about going in that direction and she hesitated about making the commitment, which also meant relocating cross-country. After all, weren't there more than enough cooking shows already all over the airwaves? Their life expectancy was projected to be somewhere a little longer than that of a common fruit fly—but not by all that much.

By then Danni had become too successful catering parties for an established clientele to want to set herself up for failure again.

She had no gimmick, she protested to the agent who had approached her with the idea of cooking before a live audience. She had nothing to set her apart from all the other chefs on TV.

"I think you're selling yourself short, Danielle," the agent, a thin, diminutive man named Baxter Warren told her with more than a little conviction. "A lot of people—the *right* people," he emphasized dramatically, "think you make desserts to die for."

As the words came out of his mouth, the agent paused for a moment, looking as if he had just had a world-altering epiphany. And then his thin lips split into a wide smile.

"That's what we'll call the show. *Danielle's Desserts to Die For.*"

"Most people call me Danni," she'd told him.

"Danni's Desserts to Die For," he amended, then nodded his head. "Even better." Baxter gave her a penetrating, almost mesmerizing look. It was easy to see that he was exceedingly pleased with himself. "You *can't* say no."

She didn't.

Danni had packed up her pots—Baxter told her she could buy a complete designer set of new ones once she landed in Southern California, but she'd insisted on bringing the ones that she'd been using. The ones her father had given her before she'd even hit her teens. They had belonged to her grandmother and to Danni the pots were the very embodiment of family history. They represented who and what she was.

She'd also brought along a box full of recipes. Recipes that she habitually—and unconsciously—augmented each time she prepared them.

With her prized possessions safely packed away, Danni had flown from Atlanta to begin a new life in the land of endless summers and endless beaches: Southern California. The cable station where her half-hour program was scheduled to be filmed was located in Burbank. Baxter had encouraged her to find either an apartment or a house in the area.

But the pace in Burbank was too frantic for her and she longed for something a little more sedate and laid-back, as well as a town that was a little less populated. What she was looking for was something to remind her of the Atlanta suburb that she'd left behind.

She was searching for a little bit of home in a completely unfamiliar environment.

She found what she was looking for in Bedford, with the help of a Realtor one of the cameramen working on her new show had recommended.

Maizie Sommers.

Moreover, Maizie, with her low key approach, her soft voice and especially her kind smile, reminded her a great deal of the mother she'd lost years ago.

What Danni appreciated most of all was that her association with Maizie was *not* terminated when escrow closed. When the woman urged her to call if she ever had a problem or needed anything—or just to talk, Danni believed her.

As a matter of fact, they'd talked several times since Danni had sent out her change-of-address postcards to the people back in Atlanta and Danni had even dropped by the woman's office a couple of times, always bearing some sort of new dessert she was currently trying out.

For her part, Maizie never put her off or told her she'd come at a bad time. On the contrary, she'd greeted her like a long-lost, beloved family member—like a daughter.

"You do realize that just the pleasure of your company would be more than enough," Maizie told her when she'd dropped by a week ago. "You really don't need to bribe me—although, I must say, you really outdid yourself this time with these little glazed Bundt cakes." Maizie had sat at her desk, examining the mini cake in her hand from all angles. It appeared perfect from all sides. "Have you thought about either writing a cookbook or marketing these? You'll make a fortune," Maizie prophesized.

Danni had modestly demurred, but the idea about writing a cookbook remained in the recesses of her brain. *Maybe someday.*

Each time she reflected on the changes that had come into her life in such a short amount of time, it always astounded her. She could hardly believe that at long last, there was enough money in both her savings and her checking account for her to be a little—hell, a *lot* extravagant if she wanted to be, instead of always having to count pennies, constantly be vigilant and deny herself even the smallest of indulgences.

Danni almost gave in to the cliché to pinch herself. Life was *that* perfect. For the first time in her life, she was living in her own house, a house she'd paid for, not a house she was merely renting and that belonged to someone else.

The rush she felt when she put the key into the lock of her own front door for the very first time was one she couldn't even begin to describe. It was unequal to anything else she'd ever felt.

But Danni wasn't so enamored with the idea of ownership that she was blind to the house's flaws. She wasn't. She was very aware that the house came with warts. Quite a few warts.

The two-story building, built somewhere around the early 1970s, was in need of a new roof, new windows that kept the air out, not invited it in, and the three bathrooms were all but literally begging to be remodeled.

The kitchen, which to her had always been the heart of the house, needed a complete makeover as well. To anyone else, these might have been a deal breaker, but Danni had fallen in love with the layout and had bought the house for an exceptionally good price. So she'd signed on the dotted line, promising herself that if and when her show's option was picked up and renewed, and *if* it subsequently took off, she would give the house a much-needed facelift.

That day had come.

Her last visit to Maizie had been to tell the helpful Realtor that she was finally at a place where she could afford all those renovations they had talked about.

"What I need now," she'd said over an enticing small pyramid of a dozen glazed wine cupcakes, "is for you to recommend a reliable general contractor who can do it all. I really don't want to have to deal with a half a dozen or more men, all at odds with one another."

There'd been a slight problem with her request. The man Maizie had been sending people to for the last eight years had recently relocated to Nevada to be closer to his daughter and her family. Consequently, Maizie had told her she'd be on the look-out for someone reliable and that she would get back to her as quickly as she could.

Danni had no doubts that the woman would find someone.

And Maizie had.

When she came home yesterday, bone weary after a marathon taping session, the first thing she'd seen was the red light on her answering machine blinking rhythmically as if it was flirting with her. Danni had stopped only long enough to drop her purse and step out of her shoes before listening to the message.

She waited less than that to call Maizie back. Five minutes after that, she was on the phone, dialing the number that Maizie had given her.

Danni wanted to call while her lucky streak was still riding high. There was a part of her—a diminishing but still-present part—that expected she would wake from this wonderful dream, her alarm clock shattering the stillness and calling her to work at the insurance company back in Atlanta.

Before that happened, she wanted to take full advantage of this magic-carpet ride she found herself on.

The man who Maizie had recommended sounded nice on the phone. He had a deep, rich baritone voice that was made for long walks on the beach beneath velvety, dark, star-lit skies.

He looked even better, Danni thought as she brought her vehicle to a squealing stop in her driveway and all but leaped out of her car. He was on time, she noted ruefully. And she was not.

"Sorry," Danni declared, approaching the man who looked as if the stereotypical description of "tall, dark and handsome" had been coined exclusively for him. She put her hand out. "Traffic from Burbank was a bear," she apologized.

His fingers closed around her hand, his eyes never leaving hers.

Stone had been all set to leave.

He absolutely hated being kept waiting and felt that

the people who were late had no regard for anyone else's time and no respect for them, either.

But the attractive, bubbly blonde's apology sounded genuine enough rather than just perfunctory and it wasn't as if he were awash in projects and could turn his back and walk away from this one.

So far, it had been a very lean year for him and the savings he'd put aside to see himself and his daughter—and sister if need be—through were just about gone.

Danni suddenly paused just as she was about to unlock her door. She half turned and looked at him over her shoulder as a thought occurred to her that she had just taken his identity for granted.

"You are Mr. Scarborough, right?" she asked belatedly, punctuating her question with a warm, hopeful smile.

Even if he wasn't, Stone caught himself thinking, he would have temporarily changed his name just to be on the receiving end of that smile. But, with a clear conscience, he could nod and say his full name, just in case the woman had any lingering doubts.

"Call me Stone," he told her. There, that should set her mind at ease about his identity. After all, he reasoned, how many men were there with that first name?

"I'm Danni," she said, her smile all but branding him. "But then, you already know that." There was just the slightest hint of pink tint on her cheek as she turned away.

She opened the front door and despite the fact that it was July and the sun had yet to go down, the interior of the house was all but utterly enshrouded in darkness.

"The first thing I'm going to need is light," she told him.

"That usually happens when you turn up the switch," he pointed out dryly, indicating the one that was on the wall right next to the doorjamb.

Danni laughed then, even as she did exactly as he'd suggested. "I mean light from above." She pointed toward the roof, which was some eighteen feet up, thanks to cathedral ceilings. "Like a skylight. This room appears incredibly gloomy in the winter, even when the drapes are opened. And I'd really rather not have to leave the lights on all day long."

As she spoke, Danni dropped her purse near the front door and saw him looking. "I could use a small table there," she admitted. "Haven't gotten around to that, yet. Haven't gotten around to a lot of things yet," she admitted ruefully in a moment of truth. "They said the pace here in Southern California is laid-back." Danni just shook her head about that. "They lied."

"They?" he asked, curious.

"The people back East."

There it was again, that accent he couldn't quite pin down. This was probably his one chance to ask her the question.

"How far back East?" he asked.

"Atlanta." She saw the look that came over his face. He assumed a triumphant air, as if he was congratulating himself on a guess well played. "Is it that obvious?"

"No, not *that* obvious," he told her. "Just that you weren't from around here."

She laughed shortly, thinking of the people she'd been

interacting with since she'd transplanted herself. She had the kind of face and manner that drew people to her. Not only that, but it drew them out as well. People would find themselves telling her things they wouldn't even whisper into their priest's ear.

"Is anyone from around here?" It was meant to be a rhetorical question, but obviously, not for Stone.

"My wife was," he told her, then added, "and my daughter is."

Is and *was.*

Danni was instantly aware of the switch in tense.

He mentioned his daughter in the present tense, but not his wife. Did that mean he was divorced, or—?

She'd always been interested in people, in the way they felt, thought, what their background was, but she also knew that men didn't like having to answer too many questions at any given time, so she let the questions bubbling up within her all go for now.

Except for one.

"Are you hungry?" she asked Stone. "Can I get you anything?"

"No, I'm fine," he assured her.

Yes, you certainly are, she couldn't help thinking. But her Southern training couldn't accept no for an answer. It wasn't in her DNA.

"No coffee? Tea?" He shook his head at each suggestion. "How about water?" she coaxed. "Everyone likes water."

He laughed at her comment and decided he was waging a losing battle. The woman would obviously remain uneasy until she'd given him *something.*

"All right. I'll take some water," he told her, all but raising his hands over his head like a prisoner being taken into custody.

"Great," Danni declared. "Water it is. And dessert," she added in a lowered voice, talking quickly. So quickly that he had to replay the words in his head in order to realize what she'd just said. "Kitchen's this way," she told him, leading the way to the rear of the house.

"I don't need dessert," Stone told the back of her head. At the moment, it was the safest place to look. If he lowered his eyes for even a second, he knew he'd regret it. The view was far too tempting. Her hips were moving at a tempo that was all but synchronized with the beating of his heart.

"Sure you do. Everyone needs dessert," she assured him.

Reaching her final destination, Danni went straight for the refrigerator and the secret weapon she used to win everyone over.

Her dessert.

Chapter Three

This was obviously a man who did *not* like being told what to do, Danni decided as she placed the large plate of freshly made dessert on the table. When he was growing up, his mother probably had to *suggest* that he drink his milk, otherwise, she was willing to bet, he went out of his way not to touch it just to prove his independence.

In some ways, she supposed she could relate to that. While she liked being polite, she was never anyone's pushover.

Maizie Sommers had sung this man's praises, which meant that in the Realtor's experience, the contractor got an overall A rating for both the quality of his work *and* the prices he charged. That was certainly more than good enough for her, Danni thought. There was no way she wanted to antagonize the man on top of already being late for their appointment and having kept him waiting.

So Danni put on her very best smile and graciously accepted his refusal of her dessert.

"Don't worry, I won't force-feed you. But it'll be right there, waiting for you, just in case you wind up changing your mind," she told him, moving away from the table. "Okay, why don't I show you what needs doing?" she offered cheerfully.

Stone barely nodded. "That sounds like a good idea," he agreed.

Danni began to regret not wearing a sweater. Did this man take time to warm up, or was he always going to be a wee bit cooler than an artic breeze?

It wasn't that she required Stone Scarborough to ooze personality and charm, it was just that she knew the work she had in mind wasn't going to be something that could be accomplished in a day or a week—or a month, even if the man moved in to do it. Since this would be a long, drawn out process and they would be around each other for a long stretch of time—unless he had a magic wand in his arsenal or a squadron of eager elves at his disposal—she definitely didn't want to feel uncomfortable in her own home for the duration of the renovations.

That meant, quite simply, that they had to get along.

More than that, it required, in her opinion, that they liked each other, at least to a modest degree. She wasn't looking for a best friend, but neither was she looked for someone who behaved as if he might appear on the cover of *Grouches Inc., Monthly* some time in the very near future.

So, as she showed the general contractor around her two-story house, Danni did her best to break through what she viewed as his crusty outer shell, hoping against hope that she wouldn't wind up just coming up against a crusty inner shell.

"Have you been a general contractor long?" Danni asked, trying to draw him into a round of pleasant small-talk.

She actually knew the answer to her own question—she'd Googled Stone Scarborough during the very short lunch break she'd taken at the studio and found the contractor's website—but it was the first question that occurred to her. In her experience, people liked to talk about themselves. It tended to put them at ease.

"Long enough to get it right," Stone answered crisply. "I can give you references from former clients if you'd like," he offered.

It couldn't hurt, Danni thought. "I'd like," she echoed out loud.

More than his caliber of work—which, because Maizie had recommended him she assumed was top-drawer—Danni wanted to talk to the women whose houses Stone had worked on. She wanted to find out if he'd been as monotone with them as he was being with her. At least then, if his personality came across the same way with them as it did with her, she wouldn't feel as if she'd offended the man.

"Then I'll get them to you tomorrow morning," Stone promised her. "Do you want to wait until you've had a chance to look them over, or do you want to go ahead and tell me what you had in mind by way of changes for this house?"

Danni looked around for a moment, as if making up

her mind one final time before speaking. As it happened, she'd already decided and she wasn't seeking other's opinions on his work to see if he was equal to the project. She just wanted to know if he ever turned out to be a "real, live boy" or continued being as wooden as Pinocchio for the entire time he worked on their renovations.

Turning toward him, Danni summed up the answer to his question regarding the work she wanted done in one succinct word. "Everything."

Because he was waiting for an answer to the first part of his question first, her answer initially confused him. "Excuse me?"

"Everything," Danni cheerfully repeated. "I need a great many changes made to this house, from top to bottom."

Stone found that that made no practical sense at all to him. "If you want to change everything, why'd you buy the house in the first place, if you don't mind my asking?" He knew that in her position, he wouldn't have. But then, he'd come to realize that the female mind worked much differently from the male one.

For one thing, logic appeared to have little or no place in it, or in making final decisions.

"No, I don't mind," Danni replied.

From her tone, he felt she wasn't just putting on an act or pretending not to mind the personal question he'd just asked—God knew that he would have. So far, she sounded pretty guileless, considering her gender. Maybe she wasn't so typical, after all.

"I bought the place because it had a price range I could afford," she admitted honestly, "the front yard had a great orientation for my flower garden and, as they say in real estate, the house looked like it had 'a lot of potential.'"

Stone shook his head when she was finished. "That's usually real estate speak for 'the house is a real clunker.'"

"But it does have potential," Danni insisted. "I can see it." And she really could. When she walked through the fifty-year-old house, she could visualize the changes she wanted. The transformation would make the two-story house into a showplace.

Stone merely shrugged. It was her money. "If you say so," he conceded. And then he got back to something she'd said about the property's orientation. "You have a flower garden?" he asked. When he'd come up the front walk, he hadn't seen a single bud and when she'd brought him into the kitchen, he had a view of the backyard—which also barren. Where was this so-called flower garden of hers?

Her smile held promise rather than embarrassment. "Not yet. But I intend to."

Stone took a wild guess. "This is more of that 'potential' the property has, right?"

The woman practically beamed at him, as if to congratulate him that he was finally getting the hang of it. "Right."

Why did she feel as if she were on trial? Maybe he was just trying to see if she committed to this and wouldn't lose interest and send him on his way in the middle of the job. If that was what he thought, he didn't know her. Once she signed on to something, she remained committed for the duration.

For the time being, she decided to stop trying to make
a personal connection with the man and just get his
input on the house. Danni continued showing the contractor around.

Stone quietly followed the woman through the first
floor, listening to the sound of her voice as she pointed
out room after room, giving him a thumbnail summary
of what she wanted changed or added or redone in each
one.

The first floor was comprised of a living room, a
dining room, a kitchen that fed into a family room and
a slightly larger than closet-size bedroom that was located all the way in the rear, just off the family room.
The entire floor had one bathroom.

The second floor, with its wide-open staircase and
carved wooden banister, contained three more bedrooms, including the less-than-masterful "master suite."
There was a bathroom between the two bedrooms and
another bathroom within the master suite. The second
floor also had a recreational room which, she discovered when he corrected her, was called a "bonus room"
in Southern California.

Stone listened without comment as she pointed things
out, saying things like "I'd like bookshelves all along
that wall" when they were in the bonus room, and "a
walk-in closet here would be nice," in the master bedroom. He neither nodded, nor said a word one way or
another until the "tour" was over and they came back
downstairs to the kitchen.

Unable to endure the man's silence any longer, Danni
finally asked, "Well? What do you think? You haven't

said a single word during the whole tour." Did that mean he wasn't going to take the job? Was she just wasting her time with him?

"You were right," he replied quietly.

She watched him, waiting for him to continue. Right? Right about what? She'd done a lot of talking in the last twenty minutes.

"Yes?" she asked.

"When you said 'everything.'" He'd thought she was kidding at the time, but it was obvious that she had to be serious. Every room needed to be redone in order to make it more useful, more pleasing to the eye and part of the twenty-first century.

He had one all-encompassing suggestion for her. "You just might be better off tearing everything down and starting from scratch."

"Not everything," Danni protested. "I actually do like the fireplace in the living room, and the staircase. And the balcony in the rec— The bonus room," she corrected herself.

In response, she saw what looked like a hint of a smile on his lips. At least she'd managed to make a very slight connection, Danni congratulated herself. It looked like the man *was* human, after all. And that meant that there *was* hope. Maybe they would be able to get along in the long run.

She crossed her fingers.

Stone watched her for a long moment. Just as she was going to ask what he was thinking, he said, "You like the balcony, huh?"

The feature, visible from the street, was what had attracted her to the house in the first place. That and the colors it'd been painted: gray and Wedgwood-blue. Like her parents' house had been, back in Atlanta. It made her a little homesick to see it, even though the actual structure looked nothing like her old home.

"Yes," she responded, then after a beat, asked, "You don't?"

He dismissed the appendage under discussion with a wave of his hand. "Well, since the balcony doesn't look out onto anything but the cul-de-sac and the house across the street, I was going to suggest you close that up and extend the bonus room by the balcony's square footage."

Danni rolled the idea over in her head, trying to picture a large window rather than the two sliding-glass doors currently there. The glass doors separated the bonus room from the balcony. The latter ran the width of the room, which in turn was the length of two of the three garages. Because the bonus room ended over the second garage, the third one had never been finished. Something else she wanted Stone to add to his list. She wanted the garage to be finished and to have an attic put in, complete with stairs that folded out onto the garage floor.

"It's worth considering," she told him. "I'll think about it."

The balcony would continue to thrive, he could see it in her eyes. He had one more suggestion for her. "It might be less expensive if you just sell this place and get something more to your liking."

She looked at him, confused. Didn't he *want* the

work? "Are you trying to talk your way out of a job, Mr. Scarborough?"

He didn't say yes, he didn't say no. "Just wanted you to be aware of all the possibilities." He paused, letting that sink in and then informed her, "All those suggestions you made during the tour, they're not going to come cheap."

How dumb did he think she was? "I didn't expect them to. That's why I waited before looking into having it done until my contract was renewed," she told him. "I wanted to be sure the money was there before I started to undertake all this."

That was commendable, Stone thought. He'd seen far too many people who harbored grandiose plans, only to allow themselves to get overextended and in over their heads when they neglected to take escalating prices and building costs into account.

He took another long look at her. The woman might look like one of those fluffy blondes who seemed to be almost everywhere you looked in Southern California—most of them would-be actresses—but she seemed to have a head on her shoulders.

Maybe they *would* be able to work things out, after all.

"When would you want me to get started?" Stone asked, then added a coda. "Provided, of course, that the estimate that I'm going to work up for you doesn't turn your hair gray."

As he talked, she subtly directed him back toward the kitchen table—where the coffee she'd made and the dessert she'd left were still waiting for them.

"I'm sure it won't," she told him. "And even if it did, there're enough hair-care products out there to restore my hair to its natural shade," she assured him with an easy, unself-conscious laugh. "Ms. Sommers seemed really sold on you and I trust her judgment implicitly. And I really liked what I saw on your website," she added for good measure. "Some of those before-and-after photos were absolutely incredible." That had really impressed her and confirmed the man's abilities.

Stone had always believed in doing the best possible job he could, bar none, but he'd never been very comfortable being on the receiving end of praise. Now was no different.

He shrugged off her words, and murmured, "My sister was the one who put together the website," as if that were enough to deflect the compliment and allow him to remain anonymously in the shadows.

"Your sister," Danni echoed. The information didn't diminish her response to his work and actually enhanced it slightly, expanding it in another direction. A direction she naturally followed.

"So, it's a family business?" Danni assumed.

"No" was his first response, but then he reconsidered. He had to admit that in the last couple of years or so, Virginia had become exceedingly involved in helping him run his construction company—in more ways than just one. "Well, actually, yes in a way," he amended. "Virginia put together that website and she handles the accounting end of the business."

Initially, Virginia had done freelance accounting for several small businesses in the area, his among them.

But of late, his business had been taking up more and more of his sister's time. It would be nice, he caught himself thinking, to be able to pay her accordingly.

If this woman was serious about two-thirds of the things she said she wanted done to her house, he could afford to pay Virginia more money—not that she ever asked for more. That wasn't her way—but he knew he'd be lost without her, not because of her accounting—or the fact that she had put together that website behind his back which, lucky for her, had turned out well—but because she was always there to help him with Ginny.

If not for Virginia, he would have had to resort to turning over Ginny's care to complete strangers and he didn't like the idea of people who weren't family or friends looking after his little girl. Especially since Ginny was not all that easy on some people's nerves. Strangers—even strangers who were paid for the job—were not always all that patient.

Virginia was.

"That sounds pretty much like a family business to me," Danni was saying, unaware that there was a wistful smile on her lips. She would have given anything to have a brother or sister around to work with, to be there for them—and have them be there for her. She had some cousins, a couple who had relocated here as a matter of fact, but it wasn't the same thing. "You have any other family?" she asked.

What was with all these non-work-related questions? "Why?" he asked.

"No reason," Danni replied with an innocent shrug.

"Just curious. I guess I just like knowing things about the people I'm dealing with."

Stone had momentarily been captivated by the movement of her shoulders as they rose and fell in an innocent shrug.

But he came to fast enough.

"All you need to know is that I take pride in my work and I stand behind everything I do," he informed her.

The woman nodded in response, then continued looking at him without saying a word. It was against his better judgment, but he decided there was no real harm in it, either. So he told her what she was obviously waiting to hear for reasons that completely escaped him.

"I have a daughter. Ginny. She's four," he added, "going on forty."

The smile he received in return made the surrender of this small piece of information oddly worth it.

"My father used to say the same thing about me," Danni recalled fondly. He'd always followed it up by telling her to slow down, that there was no hurry, the years would all be waiting for her no matter how long she would take to reach them.

"Well, my condolences to your father, then," Stone told her. There wasn't so much as a sliver of a smile as he said that.

Danni's own smile didn't appear to waver, but when he looked closer, Stone realized that what he was seeing was pain etched into the edges of that smile. She was far too young for that sort of pain.

"Too late for that," she told him. "He passed on a few years ago."

"Oh, sorry to hear that," Stone told her stiffly. Then, to his surprise and horror, he heard himself saying, "Ginny's mother did, too."

He had absolutely no idea what possessed him to share that with her. Only that it somehow seemed appropriate at the moment.

Rather than gush or give him empty platitudes the way he expected, the woman whose house he'd just finished touring and whose table he was currently sitting at, reached over and placed her hand on his. The soft, gentle, fleeting contact seemed to convey the level of her sorrow, their common *shared* sorrow, far better than a battalion of words ever could have.

"Are you raising her by yourself?" she asked. There was compassion in her voice.

Sometimes it felt that way, but that was unfair. Virginia dealt with Ginny far more than he did—unless he was between jobs and had the time to spend with Ginny. "My sister moved in to help when my wife died."

"Your sister the accountant who does your website?" she asked just to keep the details straight.

The smattering of a smile grew just for a moment before returning to a neutral expression. "That's her."

Danni smiled broadly again. "Then it really is a family business, isn't it?"

He considered the situation for a moment, then realized he had no idea why he was fighting the concept so stringently. He wouldn't have been able to take on any new jobs if it hadn't been for Virginia. At the same time, his sister had placed her life and her own business pretty much on hold because of him.

That needed to change.
Soon.
Just not yet.

Chapter Four

"What do you mean you can't watch Ginny for me?" Stone stared at his sister in utter disbelief. He'd been *counting* on Virginia. There *was* no back-up plan for him to turn to. "I'm supposed to be start working on that woman's house today. The one who cooks things," he added by way of a description in case Virginia didn't remember who he was referring to.

Virginia was caught between feeling guilty over lying to Stone and putting him through this—even if it *was* for his own good—and trying desperately to suppress the laugh bubbling up in her throat in response to what her brother assumed for an enlightening description. Leave it to Stone to reduce a notable, thriving career and identify it in such a way that it could fit just about every single woman both he and she knew—excluding

herself since she had yet to learn how to successfully
boil water without burning something.

But, for the sake of playacting—and the fact that Maizie thought that it would be in everyone's best interest
to have Stone acquaint Danni with Ginny at the very
outset of this relationship, Virginia pretended to be a
little confused.

"Are you talking about the woman with the cable network cooking show?" she asked innocently.

"Yes, her. The one whose house is going to pay for
Ginny's college education," he underscored. Stone was
only half kidding.

Danni Everett had said yes to his estimate, but not
until after asking some rather surprisingly intelligent
questions. He'd been rather impressed by that. Truthfully, he preferred working for people who had some
sort of understanding about what was involved in making the renovations they wanted and were aware that he
couldn't just mumble some incantations under his breath
and make their requested changes happen overnight. He
also appreciated that she fully understood and accepted
the fact that the house was going to look considerably
worse before it looked better. A lot of people he'd done
work for had taken exception to that.

But none of that was going to happen if he couldn't
go over there and get started.

"I'm going to college?" Ginny asked in surprise.

Stone paused to kiss the top of Ginny's head. He
kept forgetting that she listened to everything rather
than tuned conversations out, the way that most kids
Ginny's age did.

"Yes, someday," he told her. "It just might be a little harder without this new project coming through." He eyed Virginia accusingly. How could she let him down like this, without any warning? "I thought you said you'd be able to watch her for me."

They had an agreement. Since this was summer, Ginny wasn't in school—not that he considered kindergarten actually "school." But the teacher had been nice and Ginny had been with kids her own age, so that gave both of them time to conduct their business. Once the official school year started for Ginny, one of them would pick her up in the afternoon and look after the little girl.

If he was in between projects, he always made a point of being the one there for Ginny. Virginia was there the rest of the time, whenever he wasn't available. That, to him, was the beauty of his sister running her business out of the house.

With school out, Ginny had to be watched full time. For the most part, this last month, that responsibility had fallen to Virginia. There were two more months to get through and then Ginny would be going back to school, this time to first grade and that entailed longer hours, giving them both a little more time to attend to their own work.

But they weren't there just yet.

"I know and I'm sorry," Virginia apologized, doing her best to look properly contrite. "But that was before this thing came up."

"Thing?" he repeated, no more enlightened than he

had been a moment ago. "What 'thing' are we talking about?" Stone pressed.

His sister hadn't said anything to him about there being any possible snags when they'd discussed his taking on this latest job. Why had she waited until the last possible moment to throw this curve ball at him?

Virginia shrugged self-consciously. She really hadn't considered the possibility of getting the third degree when she'd begged off. She hadn't thought a plausible alibi properly through.

"A *thing*," she repeated more forcefully. "I've got this *thing*."

The annoyance over being broadsided like this by Virginia at the eleventh hour temporarily faded as Stone looked at his sister with growing concern.

"There's nothing wrong, is there, Virginia?" he asked, all sorts of horrible possibilities running through his mind. After all, Eva had been healthy and thriving until suddenly, her life ended. He knew firsthand how quickly fate could strike, canceling out a life. "You're not going to see a doctor or anything like that, are you, Virginia?" he asked, his voice pulsing with growing concern.

Virginia was exceedingly tempted to grab the excuse he'd just handed her on a silver platter, but she knew Stone. If he thought there was anything wrong with her, if he even *suspected* that she was ill, he'd put his own entire life on hold and insist on going with her to the doctor, or specialist, and he'd want to be right there, in the office to discuss her options and offer her his physical and emotional support.

He could be incredibly selfless at times, but she felt

he was letting that sterling quality go to waste on her. Somewhere out there—hopefully a lot closer to home— there was a woman who needed a man like Stone—and who could be the kind of woman that *he* needed as well.

What she needed right now, for both their sakes, was a plausible excuse he could accept, one that would cause him to back off.

The "thing" could be a new client, she suddenly thought. Quickly, her brain scrambled to come up with some details—*any* sort of details—to toss her brother's way.

Specifics continued to elude her.

She went with vague. "I've got this new client I'm trying to land. They said they wanted to meet with me for an early lunch. If things go well, it might turn out to be a very *long* lunch," she told him. "I just can't take the munchkin with me."

Stone nodded. "No, you can't," he agreed.

"Hey, I've got an idea," Virginia said brightly. "Why don't you take her with you?"

"As what?" Had Virginia lost her mind? "My assistant?" he asked with a touch of sarcasm.

"Sure, Daddy, I can be your assistant," Ginny piped up excitedly, enunciating the last word very carefully. "I can help. Like when you were fixing the leak in the kitchen. Remember?"

He remembered. The leak had taken him twice as long to stop, but he hadn't wanted to discourage Ginny's desire to be helpful. He couldn't afford to take that kind of time on a customer's house, otherwise, he'd be there until Ginny graduated high school.

"I remember, honey. But that was our leak and our kitchen," he pointed out.

Her eyebrows drew together in consternation. "The lady doesn't like little kids helping to fix leaks?" she asked him.

Stone looked at her, caught off guard by something she'd just said. "Ginny, how did you know my new client is a lady?" To the best of his recollection, he hadn't said anything to his daughter about the woman.

Unlike her aunt, Ginny seemed to have an answer for everything. "I heard you talking to Aunt Virginia about her," Ginny told him innocently.

"I really don't remember saying anything," Stone told his daughter as he tried to recall what Ginny could have overheard. Giving up, he shrugged. "Not important," he decided. "However, I'd better call to tell her I won't be able to get started today."

But as he reached into his pocket to extract his cell phone, Ginny caught his hand, pulling it toward her. "No, don't, Daddy. You can go see the lady. I'm a big girl. I can stay home alone until you get back. I'm brave," she added as a final convincing argument, lifting her chin up proudly.

Touched, Stone laughed as he ruffled her hair. "Nice try, kiddo—and don't think I don't appreciate this— but you're not quite old enough to be home alone." She began to protest, but he cut her off before she could say anything. "Besides, you get into trouble just being in a room alone, never mind a house."

"But Daddy—" Ginny began, this time sounding far

more urgent than the first time she'd attempted to convince him she could remain alone.

"Quiet, kiddo," he chided. "I'm dialing." Stone nodded at the card he had in front of him as he tapped out the numbers. The phone rang only once. And then he heard the phone on the other end of the line being picked up. He really hoped the woman was as reasonable as she looked. "Ms. Everett?" he asked once he heard the melodious greeting on the other end.

Danni recognized his voice immediately. She also recognized that tiny little flip her stomach had made. A tiny little flip it had no business making.

"Stone."

The way she said his name brought an instant feeling of warmth rushing over him. Since when had his imagination taken on this extra dimension? His imagination had always been restricted to envisioning projects, not anything else.

"Today's the day you're going to get started, isn't it?" he heard her saying. "I didn't get my dates confused, did I?" she asked him.

"No, you didn't, but about that," he began, taking advantage of the segue, each word weighing heavily on his tongue, "I'm afraid I'm going to have to cancel today."

"Oh." He heard genuine disappointment throbbing in her voice and he was sorry about that. Still, he wasn't prepared for what came next. She asked him "Why?" Ordinarily, when delays cropped up—and they did on rare occasions, usually involving a delay in the primary materials arriving—the people he was working for at the time never asked *why* he wasn't coming, they just accepted that he wasn't.

"My sitter canceled at the last minute," he told Danni, sparing Virginia a less than pleased glance, "and I've got no one to watch my daughter. It'll take me time to make other arrangements, so I thought it might be best if I just—"

"Bring her with you," Danni interjected the invitation before he could finish his sentence.

Stone halted abruptly, caught completely off guard. He was certain that he'd misheard the woman on the other end of the line.

"Excuse me?"

"Bring her with you," Danni repeated, then added, "Your daughter," so that there was no wiggle room for misunderstanding. "Look, I had my producer rework the taping schedule so I that could take the day off and be here—in case you had any concerns or questions that suddenly occurred to you when you got started on the house," she explained. "Since I'm going to be here for the day, you might as well take advantage of that."

For a second, it sounded like an invitation to him, but he knew she couldn't possibly mean what he thought she was saying. "Are you saying that you're volunteering to take care of my daughter for me today while I work on your house?"

"That's exactly what I'm saying."

He could have sworn he heard a smile in her voice. And he would have been lying if he pretended not to be tempted by what she was proposing. Still, he knew he couldn't agree to it. This arrangement would somehow bend the rules—wouldn't it?

"I can't ask you to do that," he told her.

"Well," she began slowly, "as I remember this conversation—you didn't. I'm volunteering," Danni pointed out. "I'm really pretty good with kids." Then, in case he needed convincing, she continued, "I've got a goddaughter who's just a little older than Ginny and I've taken her to the amusement park a few times without losing her or breaking her."

"How do you know how old my daughter is?" Stone asked, still somewhat stunned that his client was offering to help out like this.

"You told me," she reminded him. "The first time we met. You said she was four, going on forty," Danni repeated the phrase he'd used. "Remember?"

"Now I do."

He remembered the whole exchange. Remembered thinking that she had drawn the information out of him because he was talking more than he was accustomed to with a client. Stone found himself feeling rather awkward and foolish about the whole episode—and he wasn't altogether certain as to why.

"Then you'll bring her over?" Danni asked, clearly pleased by what she assumed his answer would be. "I would really love to have you get started on the house and I'm sure I can keep your daughter occupied for the duration that you're here."

Stone paused, giving her offer some genuine consideration. He knew he could ask Ginny to be on her very best behavior and she would promise him she would be and she'd actually mean it. But there was absolutely no denying that the diminutive girl was a live wire, one that couldn't readily be contained, or entertained in hopes that she would be mesmerized enough to actually remain still.

Still, he heard himself asking, "You're sure about this?"

He had no desire to wind up losing a client because he didn't want to postpone his starting date.

"Absolutely," Danni said with feeling. "I'd love to meet her."

Careful what you wish for, lady, he warned her silently. Out loud, he said with more than a trace of skepticism, "Okay, I'll bring Ginny with me. But at the first sign that my daughter's getting to be too much for you, I want you to let me know and I'll take her right home."

Danni sensed that protesting she was perfectly equal to anything a four-year-old had in her bag of tricks wouldn't convince the stoic contractor one bit and would just be a colossal waste of time, as well as her breath.

So instead, she replied complacently, "I'll let you know."

"All right. We'll be over soon," he said, ending the call.

The woman wasn't going to let him know if Ginny got to be too much for her, he thought, putting his cell phone away. He could just *feel* it in his bones. Something about the woman struck him as being much too stubborn to admit to being tired out by a four-year-old.

He looked at his daughter doubtfully, then glanced

over at his sister again. "You're absolutely certain that you can't—"

"Absolutely certain," Virginia echoed his words, cutting him off. "As a matter of fact, I should be getting ready to go right now." About to leave the room and run up the stairs to her bedroom, Virginia paused to kiss the top of Ginny's head and to issue the little girl a warning. "Remember, I want you to be on your best behavior, Munchkin."

"I will, Aunt Virginia," Ginny promised.

Virginia eyed her niece, not completely convinced she'd gotten through to her. Ginny was just too exuberant for anyone's own good.

"Remember what's at stake," she reminded the little girl. In response, Ginny nodded her head solemnly and vigorously.

"What's at stake?" Stone asked, wondering if his sister and his daughter had some sort of code worked out between them. It seemed like an odd choice of words to use.

"My college education," Ginny immediately piped up, then looked at him expectantly. "You said so, remember, Daddy?"

Virginia turned away so her brother wouldn't see her smile. Ginny had the makings of a great little spy someday, she couldn't help thinking.

"I remember," Stone answered.

He looked from his pint-size offspring to his sibling. Something was up, he could swear to it. But for the life of him, he had no idea what it could be, or how to even begin to frame his question so he could ask the two of

them what was going on. He knew they'd feign innocence and ask him what he meant—and he wouldn't be
able to tell them, or go into any sort of an explanation,
other than to say that something just felt…off.

So for now, Stone decided just let it go and hope for
the best.

"Okay, Gin, go pack up a few of your toys and let's
go," he told his daughter.

"Be right back, Daddy," she promised, flying out of
the room. He looked after her, mystified.

Definitely something off, he thought.

He was more convinced than ever when Ginny returned almost immediately, her backpack bulging with
her favorite toys.

It was almost, he speculated, as if she had them already packed and waiting.

Why would she do that?

The answer was she wouldn't. After all, she was only
four, he reminded himself, and that sort of thing would
have taken a little planning on her part. Four-year-olds—
even those who were almost five, like Ginny, didn't plan
anything.

Still, he commented, "That was fast," just to see what
she would say.

"I *am* fast, Daddy," Ginny informed him proudly,
puffing up her chest a little.

She was one of a kind, his Ginny, he couldn't help
thinking.

"And you know to be on your best behavior, right?"
he asked her even though Virginia had just said the same
thing to her less than five minutes ago.

"Right," she parroted back eagerly, then, for good measure, she crossed her heart and gave him her one-hundred-watt smile. "The bestest," she declared.

Stone nodded, trying to convince himself that he had nothing to worry about as he left the house. What was the worst thing that could happen? He supposed that his new client could quickly become his ex-new client. But he'd weathered things like that before—usually after his clients had made unreasonable demands on either a completion date, or a cost estimate.

This, Stone thought, would probably be the first time he would have a project terminated "on account of daughter."

Opening the rear passenger door to his wide-body truck, he stepped back to allow Ginny room to scramble up to her seat, then he lifted her onto the car seat he had secured there. Strapping her in, he checked to make sure the belts all held before shutting the door and then rounding the hood to get to the driver's side. He slid in behind the wheel, snapping in his own seat belt and then started up the truck.

"When can I ride shotgun in front with you, Daddy?" Ginny asked, raising her voice above the starting hum of the truck's engine.

"When your legs are long enough for your feet to touch the floor," he informed her automatically. This wasn't the first time she asked the question.

"Okay."

That sounded *much* too complacent for Ginny. Maybe, he thought as he glanced at his daughter in the rearview mirror, he should have checked his garage for a pod before he left.

But since he was already running late, "pod checking" was going to have to wait until later, when he got back, he told himself.

Until then, all he could do was pray that Ginny's good behavior somehow continued.

Chapter Five

When she was taping her cable cooking program, or meeting with the handful of business clients—she liked keeping her hand in the catering business just in case the cable program disappeared, as so many did—Danni made certain that she always dressed well. That meant wearing either attractive dresses or flattering skirts and matching tops. Either way, she always completed the outfit with killer high heels.

She usually picked the heels before she picked the outfit.

On her few days off, Danni did a complete about-face and dressed as casually and comfortably as possible. That translated to wearing either jeans or shorts when it was hot, accompanied by a colorful cotton T-shirt, the bottom of which usually conducted a flirtatious relationship with her midriff. And although she'd slip on a pair of mules if she was going to the mailbox or into the garage, for the most part, Danni would walk around her house and patio barefoot.

So, when Stone rang the front doorbell—after issuing one last warning to his daughter to remember to be on her very best behavior—and the door opened, he didn't recognize the barefoot female standing in the doorway at first.

The young woman looked far more like a carefree first-year college student than she did the central figure in a currently up-and-rising cable cooking program.

So much so that at first glance, Stone thought he was looking at the woman's younger cousin or maybe her kid sister. Since there didn't seem to be anyone else coming up behind the young woman, he asked, "Is Ms. Everett around? I'm Stone Scarborough and I'm supposed to start working on her house today." For emphasis, he nodded at the oversize toolbox he was holding. He took it with him to every job, a last Christmas present from his late wife.

Before the young woman in the thin sky-blue T-shirt—a T-shirt that seemed to be adhering to her torso closer than a second skin—could respond, Ginny, not to be left out, introduced herself.

"And I'm Virginia Scarborough," Ginny announced proudly to the pretty lady in the doorway. "Everybody calls me Ginny so they don't get confused between me and my aunt Virginia. You can call me Ginny, too," she told her, grinning from ear to ear. "Daddy told me you were a godmother. Does that mean you're God's mother?" Ginny asked, curious. "'Cause Aunt Virginia told me God already has a mother. Her first name's Mary, is that your first name?"

"Ginny, what did I tell you about talking too much?" Stone asked, trying to curtail his mini inquisitor, as well as his own impatience.

Ginny instantly looked down on the ground, as if that would summon a subdued nature. "Not to," she replied, mumbling the answer into her small chest.

"No," he answered patiently, "I said to remember to *breathe* in between sentences. You have to breathe, Ginny," he told her firmly. It was the only chance a person had to get a word in edgewise when his daughter started with her nonstop rhetoric.

That said, Stone raised his eyes to look at the petite, barefoot young woman. She appeared to be extremely amused by the whole scenario being acted out right in front of her.

"Sorry about that," he apologized. "Ginny tends to get carried away sometimes when she meets new people."

"Nothing to be sorry about," Danni assured him. She smiled warmly at the little girl. "I understand completely."

Ginny's eyes were all but shining.

"You do?" she asked, clearly thrilled and stunned at the same time.

"Absolutely. Sometimes I get so excited about something new, I don't know what to say first, so all the words seem to come tumbling out all at once, and they even get tangled up sometimes," Danni told her as solemnly as she could manage.

Ginny was literally beaming, Stone noted, as the little girl turned to momentarily look back at him. "She's nice, Daddy."

Danni suppressed a delighted laugh. "Glad I passed inspection." And then she looked at Stone. "And I do know who you are, Mr. Scarborough," she assured him. "We met when you came by to see my house and to work up an estimate after I told you what I wanted done. You told me I might want to consider buying another house. I didn't want to."

Amused by what she assumed was the reason for his repeated introduction, Danni said, "In case you're wondering, my memory is just fine. And the cookies that I bake just have the ingredients you can easily buy over the counter in any supermarket—nothing more," she informed him, ending her statement with a wink.

For some reason, the wink seemed to go straight to his gut.

For one of the very few times in his life—possibly the very first—Stone felt flustered. Because she looked so different from their first meeting, he didn't fully recognize the woman who would be signing his checks for a while. Maybe it was too early in the morning. Looking more closely now, he realized his mistake.

"I didn't mean to imply, that is—I didn't completely recognize you at first," Stone finally managed to say. "You look like your own kid sister," Stone added, at a loss as to how to rectify the situation and backtrack gracefully.

Was he actually telling her that she looked like a kid? The smile curving her mouth was somewhat bemused.

"I don't know if that's a good thing or a bad thing," Danni commented.

He didn't want her to think he was trying to get too personal—or flirt with her. "It's not supposed to be either, just an observation," he explained honestly.

Danni put her own interpretation to his response. "I didn't mean to make it sound as if I was fishing for a compliment," she told him. "It's just that nobody's ever said anything like that to me before, that I look too young," she added in case he wasn't following her line of thinking.

Stone thought of protesting that she didn't look too young, but that really wasn't the truth, because she did. So instead, he fell back on logic. "Do you have mirrors in the house?"

Danni blinked. "Yes, of course I do." There was one right over there, on the far wall, and she nodded toward it.

"Do you ever look in any of those mirrors when you're dressed like that?" he asked pointedly.

Aside from the shorts and clingy T-shirt, she was wearing her hair in two separate ponytails, jauntily perched high on her head. They swished back and forth as she moved. She didn't even look as if she was twenty, much less any older.

Danni looked down at her clothes, then back up again at him. She didn't need a mirror, she could just imagine that someone coming in, expecting to see the star of a new cable cooking program might think she was just some young relative hanging around.

She was also blessed with her mother's skin, which

seemed to defy age and didn't turn to leather despite her love of the outdoors—although lately, that love wasn't something she was able to indulge in very often.

She supposed, if it was a choice between looking older than she was or younger than she was, she'd choose the latter.

"Point taken," Danni told her contractor. Looking up, her wide smile was back in place. "Now, can I offer you something to eat or drink before you get started?"

He didn't believe in taking a break before getting started. Besides, he liked doing what he did and was eager to get started.

"If it's all the same to you, I'd like to begin working. Not really sure just how much time I can devote to anything today," he said, casting an apprehensive side glance toward his daughter.

The way he looked at his daughter was not wasted on Danni.

"Don't worry about Ginny," she told him, easily taking the little girl's hand in hers. "I have a project that needs some very valuable little-girl input," she said, addressing her words to Stone as well as to his daughter.

"What's input?" Ginny asked.

"Words," Danni said simply. "I want to find out what you think of some of these new desserts I'm going to be making for my viewers."

"Cool," Ginny declared, her eyes wide enough to pass for the proverbial saucers.

"But first, I'm going to have to make the desserts. For that, I'm going to need an assistant to help me. She needs to be about this tall." Danni held her hand up to indicate approximately Ginny's height. "Would you have any idea where I can find someone like that?"

"Me!" Ginny declared, raising her hand in the air as if she were in school, trying to get the teacher's attention. "Me, I can help and be your 'sistant," she told Danni with enthusiasm.

"You?" She glanced at Ginny, pretending that she was just seeing the little girl for the first time and was seriously considering the possibility of taking her up on her offer to help. "Are you sure that you have the time to help me?" Danni asked, keeping a perfectly straight face.

"Yes! Daddy said he was going to be here at least an hour, maybe two," she told her new best friend. "Or more," she added with a whisper. "So I can be your 'sistent!"

Danni peered over the little girl's head toward the man she had hired to bring new life to her house.

"An hour or two?" she questioned. She'd expected him to be here for most of the day. Just how fast did this man work?

Stone subtly indicated his daughter with his eyes, then looked back at her. "I thought that two hours might be all you could handle."

Danni smiled then, the same smile he'd seen the other day, the one that looked as if it had enough wattage to light up a good part of the first floor in the dead of night.

"I think you might be underestimating me, Mr. Scarborough," she told him.

"Apparently," he agreed, thinking of what he had just witnessed. In a few easy words, she'd seemed to have made a friend for life out of his daughter. Danni had certainly won the little girl's heart and made her feel useful at the same time. "And it's Stone," he told her. Addressing him formally just seemed out of place in this situation. "My name," he clarified.

"Yes, I know," she replied with the same warm smile that for some reason made him feel unseasonably hot.

Stone forced himself to look away. If he didn't, there was a very real danger of his just standing there, staring at Danni, being completely mesmerized by the woman, by her smile, and by the utter unassuming power she was able to wield over his firecracker of a daughter.

"I'll just go get started," he murmured, pointing toward the door and the driveway beyond where his truck was parked.

"You do that," Danni agreed. "And my assistant and I will do the same." She looked down at the little girl. "Right, Ginny?"

"Right!" the little girl declared happily.

Even though Stone allowed himself a slight, private smile, he still couldn't help wondering if this woman knew just what she was letting herself in for. Ginny could tire out a legion of saints once she got going.

He knew that whenever either he or his sister gave Ginny a time-out, it wasn't done so that she could sit in her room, reflecting on what she'd done wrong; it was so that he and Virginia could get a little break, a breather, before they began trying to regroup and prepare for the next onslaught of Ginny, The Tireless Warrior Princess.

From what he'd observed, although Danni seemed to be energetic and she was certainly imaginative, he wasn't all that certain that the newest cable personality would be equal to not just putting up with, but surviving his daughter.

He decided to work as quickly as possible and get as much done as he could before the call for help—following Danni's complete surrender—rang out through the house.

Stone glanced at his watch.

Immersing himself in his work—which required that he completely gut the first room he'd chosen to work on, the downstairs rear bedroom—he realized that he'd apparently lost track of time. Before he knew it, more than two hours had gone by. Two hours where the only sound he'd heard were the sounds he'd created himself when he turned his power tools on and used them.

Stone stood now in the middle of the barren room, looking at what was left after he'd ripped away the plasterboard and what had once been some rather awful-looking rust-colored shag rugs. He shook his head as he regarded the pile of off-colored orangey-rust. It was incredible what bad taste an entire generation had adopted, he'd thought when he began separating the pieces of rug from the floor.

But he wasn't thinking about bad taste at the moment, or even envisioning what he would eventually turn this room into. He was concerned that he hadn't heard any sounds coming from the kitchen where his daughter and Danni were supposed to be working.

Granted the machines he was operating tended to drown most things out, but they hadn't been on nonstop.

Taking off the safety glasses he was wearing and

turning off the sander he'd been using on a particularly stubborn section of plasterboard, he left the room and went in search of his daughter. He sincerely hoped nothing was wrong and that he hadn't lost one client before he really had her, but he couldn't help having his doubts.

He needed to check on his daughter and what she'd done to Danni.

The moment he walked out of the back bedroom, he realized he could smell it. Smell a tantalizing aroma that suggested something exceptionally pleasing to the palette was going on in the oven.

As he approached the kitchen, Stone looked around and saw no one. He did detect a slight ticking sound, once he acclimated himself to what he first presumed was the silence. He quickly realized that what he was listening to was a timer. A timer that had exactly ten seconds left before it suddenly announced the end of its journey.

Rather than ring, the timer, jauntily mounted on the refrigerator, began to buzz. Buzz loudly and continuously, pulsing demandingly until someone paid attention to it, shut it off and took out whatever it was timing.

"Ginny?" he called. "Ginny, where did you go off to?" *And what have you done with Danni?*

"I'm right here, Daddy!" Ginny announced, all but bouncing into the kitchen from the direction of the living room.

Danni strode in right behind her.

Stone hadn't noticed until just now that for what was a rather petite woman, the cable channel's new cooking darling had a really long pair of legs.

A very attractive, really long pair of legs.

He caught himself staring at them as he watched Danni hurrying into the room, and for just a moment, he forgot that he'd been taught as a child that it wasn't very polite to stare.

The word *polite* really wasn't entering into the equation at all at the moment. But other words, other sensations and feelings, were.

And not exclusively for Stone.

Because even as she hurried over to the stove, Danni saw her contractor staring. And it wasn't at the stove.

A warm shiver danced down her spine.

Chapter Six

"Where were you?" Stone asked, tearing his eyes away from Danni and making a conscious effort to focus only on his daughter.

"We were in the living room," Ginny answered before Danni had a chance to explain anything to her father. "Danni's got this really awesome gaming system."

And it was crystal clear to Stone, by the look on his daughter's face, that she was absolutely enamored with the video gaming system.

And just possibly, with the owner of the gaming system as well.

"You have kids?" he asked Danni. She'd only mentioned having a goddaughter when he'd called to cancel on her because he didn't have a sitter for Ginny. Who bought a gaming system for a goddaughter who was dropped off occasionally?

Danni shook her head. "No."

His eyebrows drew together into one perplexed, wavy line. The woman certainly didn't look like a computer geek or gaming nerd. But those were the only two options that might explain why someone over the age of eighteen would have a sophisticated gaming system—or any gaming system for that matter.

"Then why do you have a gaming system in your living room?" Stone asked her.

Danni went with the very obvious: She had money and she liked pleasing a child in her life.

"Because, even though I don't have a child, I *do* have a goddaughter and she likes to play competitively. I found some age-appropriate games for her—which meant I needed a system to play them on. It also meant I had to learn how to play and hold up my end if I ever hoped to have a chance of winning." She glanced over at Ginny. "She's very sharp, your daughter."

Danni would get no argument out of him on that count. "Like I said, four going on forty."

"I'm gonna be five very soon," Ginny volunteered to Danni proudly.

"Too soon," Stone commented. He could vividly remember bringing her home from the hospital, thinking, as he held her, that she was liable to break at any second. The fear stayed with him for a while.

Ginny sniffed as she put her hands on her very small, barely noticeable little hips and told her father in the oldest voice she could muster, "I can't stay a little girl forever, you know."

Danni laughed. "Sounds like she's already on her way to growing up."

Stone sighed as he shook his head. "Don't I know it. Well, I'll take her off your hands now."

Danni looked at him in surprise. "You're finished for the day?" By her reckoning, he'd only been at it for just a little under two hours.

"I gutted one room." But that wasn't why he was getting ready to pack up and leave for the day. "I thought my daughter would have tired you out by now."

Danni laughed softly. "We Georgia girls are a lot heartier than we look," she informed him with a touch of pride.

"I like your accent," he realized. That slight lilt in her voice he heard every now and then, the comfortable way she had of talking, it had a pleasing effect on him.

Danni had tried very hard to lose her accent, paying very close attention to the cadence of those who did not drawl, twang or have a nasal intonation.

She wanted to sound like a Midwesterner.

What she definitely didn't want was for someone to think that her Georgia accent was actually a gimmick she was falling back on to distinguish her from some of the other cable channel chefs.

She had never believed in gimmicks. She wanted to appeal to everyone across the board.

"I don't have an accent," Danni protested with alacrity.

There was just the barest hint of a smile curving the corners of Stone's mouth. How could a proverbial "Georgia Peach" think she didn't have a Southern accent?

"Yes, you do," Stone countered.

Ginny looked from one adult to the other and seemed very quickly to pick a side. She backed up her new best friend loyally and even moved a little bit closer to her, taking a couple of steps in her direction.

"No, she doesn't, Daddy," Ginny pronounced solemnly. "She sounds just like you and me. Well, me anyway, 'cause you don't really do much talking, Daddy," his daughter informed him.

Danni pressed her lips together to keep back her laugh, not wanting to hurt the little girl's feelings—or offend Ginny's father.

"Looks like I have a defender," she said with a warm smile. Danni ran her hand affectionately over the little girl's curly hair. If things had gone another way, she might have had a child of her own by now, rather than just her own cooking program.

Hey, things don't always work out the way we plan, a voice in her head reminded her. *Focus on what you do have, not what you don't.*

It was an adage her father had been fond of repeating often and she had to admit that it had helped to see her through some pretty rough times in the last couple of years.

Since the woman was apparently sensitive on the subject of accents, Stone let the matter drop—except for one consequence that had raised its head during the discussion. Ginny had been really quick to come to Danni's defense. He had to admit he'd never seen his daughter take to anyone as fast as she had to this woman. Not

that Ginny was exactly shy, but this had to be a new record, even for her.

"She really seems to have taken a shine to you," he
commented to Danni.

"The feeling is more than mutual," Danni assured
both father and daughter, winking at the latter as if they
had some sort of secret between them.

Ginny was apparently eager to show her father what
they'd been up to while he'd been working. The girl
looked toward the oven that was currently housing not
just the fruit of their effects, but the really delicious
aroma that came along it.

"You wanna try the pie we made?" Ginny asked her
father, looking ready to simply leap out of her skin with
enthusiasm.

He wasn't sure whether to say yes or no, neither was
he certain if the offering *was* his daughter's to make.

"I think that Danni has other ideas for the pie." He
assumed it was going with the woman to the cable studio, to be part of her program; the "after" photograph
used to encourage people who ordinarily burned water
not to give up.

"No, I don't," Danni corrected him cheerfully. "I
thought it might be a good experience for Ginny to help
me prepare and bake a pecan pie and then find out firsthand just how good it can turn out." She looked at the
little girl, who already needed no encouragement—or
any elaborate traveling directions—to make a beeline
for the stove.

Taking a pair of embroidered pot holders from a
drawer, Danni opened the oven door and then very care-

fully removed the chocolate pecan pie. She placed it on top of the stove to cool.

Noting the eager expression on the little girl's face, Danni cautioned, "It has to cool off first, honey. If you try to sample any of it now, you'll wind up burning your tongue."

Putting her hands behind her back, Ginny rocked back on her heels and said innocently, "Wasn't gonna try to eat it now. Not even one tiny piece," she declared, holding her small thumb and forefinger up and just a sliver apart to show just how small a piece she had no intentions of having.

Thoroughly amused, Danni continued the dialogue between herself and her Muppet-size assistant. "I see that you've thought this all out very carefully, haven't you?" Danni said to her, addressing Ginny the way she would another adult.

Her method completely won over Ginny's heart. "Yes, ma'am," she agreed.

Danni finally raised her eyes to look at Ginny's father and saw the very strange expression on his face. She made no effort to try to fathom what was behind it. That would only be a waste of time.

"Is there something wrong?" she asked.

Stone shook his head, still watching his daughter. "Not a thing. I was just thinking that I'd never seen Ginny respond to anyone the way she does to you." He made no effort to hide his unabashed wonder.

That was probably because—she would have placed a silent bet on the fact that—there wasn't overly much female traffic going back and forth from Stone's house.

He appeared too serious, too wrapped up in his work, to have time for "recreational activities" she believed one of those TV fix-all pseudo doctors had called it.

"Would you like to sample a piece once it cools off?" Danni offered.

He saw no reason to demur. The aroma was causing his stomach to almost contract in anticipation. "Sure, why not?" he agreed off-handedly, then added, "But you're sure we're not in your way?"

"What 'way'?" she asked. "I'm not doing anything except talking to you—and baking with a really good assistant," she added, flashing a wide smile at Ginny. "And for the record, if you feel like maybe doing a little more—gutting, is it?" Danni asked, referring to what he'd just told her he'd just finished doing to her back bedroom.

Stone nodded, confirming the term she'd just used.

"If you feel like doing a little more gutting today, there is another dish I thought that my willing assistant and I could try our hands at—but only if you have some work to do," she stipulated.

He had, technically, the whole house to work on. He just had to pick a spot. "You could make one hell of a negotiator, you know?" he said to her, then let her know that he had plenty of rooms to choose from for his next gutting.

"Sure," he told her agreeably. "If you really have more to do and my daughter's 'assisting' you hasn't pushed you over the edge yet—"

"It hasn't," she quickly interjected, not wanting to give Ginny anything remotely scary to think about late at night. "And it won't," she added with certainty, earning the little assistant's undying love right then and there.

"Then yeah, okay, I can do some more gutting," he agreed. "I thought that I'd do the bathroom off the back bedroom next, unless you'd rather I did another area instead."

That happened to be the only bathroom on the first floor. She decided that perhaps a question regarding timing might be in order right about here.

"How long between when you gut them and put them back into working order?" she asked.

Stone thought about it for a moment. He had no intentions of being vague or promising something he wouldn't be able to deliver on.

"Well, that really all depends on the size of the room that we're talking about," Stone qualified.

"The bathroom," Danni reminded him, nodding in the general direction of the room he'd told her he would do next.

That bathroom was considered a three-quarter model since there was no tub, only a shower. "I'd say about three, four days tops."

That sounded reasonable to her. She could certainly put up with that time frame. Going up and down the stairs more frequently was good for her, Danni told herself. It forced her to exercise her legs, never a bad thing.

Danni nodded her approval then said, "Go for it," out loud.

Stone didn't have to be told twice.

As he left the kitchen, in the background, he heard his daughter ask, "What are we gonna make next?"

"How do you feel about chicken potpie?" Danni asked her.

"I don't know," Ginny confessed honestly. "What is it?"

He didn't see the woman's smile, but he heard it in her voice. Though his back was to Danni just as he went into the hall, the smile in her voice had brought out one in kind to his lips.

"Absolutely delicious," Danni told her.

That was more than good enough for Ginny. "I like delicious," Ginny told her. "Let's make it!" she cried with enthusiasm and anticipation.

Stone picked up his sledge hammer and went back to work, marveling about what he'd just witnessed.

No matter how good a pastry chef the petite, sexy blonde was, she was really wasting her time at it. From the little bit he'd witnessed today, he could swear that Danielle Everett could be a really great child whisperer.

In the limited amount of time the woman had been with Ginny, she all but had the little girl wrapped around her little finger, ready to do anything she suggested.

He'd never seen anything like it before.

The tempting aroma of the cooling pie seemed to follow him all the way to the rear of the house. He could almost feel his mouth watering.

As he closed the door to minimize the noise of what he was about to do, he also deliberately sealed himself away from the tempting aroma that was wafting from the kitchen.

Even so, with the door closed and the aroma presumably barred from entering, he found that his mouth wouldn't stop watering.

He worked faster.

He had no other choice.

When Stone was finished and made his way back into the kitchen some ninety minutes later, he was rather spent and convinced that he now smelled far too gamey for mixed company. His new plan was to collect his daughter and go home, certain that by now Ginny had probably worn through all of the woman's steady nerves and that Danni in turn would be more than happy to see his truck pulling out of her driveway with Ginny strapped into the rear passenger seat, in a car seat.

"Daddy!" Ginny cried eagerly when she saw him coming into the room. "Are you finished for real this time?"

"I'm finished for real this time," he echoed instead of immediately telling his daughter that they were going home.

He saw the eager expression on his daughter's face. Was that due to what she'd been doing these last ninety minutes? Most likely it was, which made the woman with her nothing short of a real miracle worker.

Ginny ran up to him, no doubt very excited about what she'd been doing these last few hours. She moved in to hug him, then abruptly stopped and wrinkled her nose.

She gazed up at him with horror. "You smell funny, Daddy."

"That's just the scent of honest toil," Danni called out to Ginny from the far side of the kitchen. She was rummaging through the refrigerator. "Right?" she asked, making eye contact with Stone.

"Right," he agreed.

At least she wasn't wrinkling her nose at him, he thought. Whenever Elizabeth was around him right after he finished up a job, she'd flatly tell him that he needed to clean up first before he did anything else. Especially if he intended to do it around her.

"I'll just take Ginny and we'll get going," he told Danni.

"But, Daddy, you have to try what we've been making first. Danni said it was a late lunch. Your reward for all that hard work you did."

It was obvious that Ginny was quoting the woman, her new idol.

"I don't think that Danni wants to be around someone who smells like a barn," Stone said, trying to usher his daughter toward the front door.

"'Danni' knows how to make herself heard if she wants to," Danni informed him with an amused smile, as she walked toward him and his daughter. "However, if you feel uncomfortable about being a wee bit, um, sweaty," she said tactfully, "you're more than welcome to take a shower in one of the bathrooms upstairs. Ginny and I will wait until you come down again before eating," she promised. "Won't we, Ginny?"

"You bet!" Ginny cried.

"You're serious?" he asked Danni.

"Of course I'm serious. I can stop smiling and say it again with a frown if that would be more convincing,"

Danni offered, doing her best to suppress the grin trying to steal over her lips.

A shower would help, but that wasn't the total answer. "Even if I take a shower, my clothes aren't exactly fresh."

"There're some clothes in a box in one of the upstairs bedrooms. You can't miss it. The box is in the middle of the room. You might find something there that'll fit you."

That sounded a bit odd to him.

"You just happen to have some spare men's clothing that *might* fit me?" he asked incredulously.

The clothes had been some of the last ones she'd bought her father. Up until now, she hadn't been able to force herself to give them away to some charity where they would do some good.

But she'd finally crossed that sentimental hurdle and was ready to move on—to some extent. However, she didn't really want to go into any of that in detail, at least not yet.

"I just happen to be packing them up to give to charity. They're all still in good condition. I think they're pretty much your size." Her father had been a big man. He'd always made her feel safe, that nothing bad could happen to her while she was with him.

She only wished that it had worked in reverse.

"Feel free to take anything you find there," she added.

He still hesitated, not wanting to take anything away from someone else if they were in greater need than he was.

But then Ginny delivered the winning argument. "Go, take a shower, Daddy. So you can come back down and taste the yummy stuff Danni taught me to make. Hurry, Daddy, before it gets all cold."

Danni smiled at him. "I believe you have your orders, *Daddy.*"

He nodded and hurried away, absently wondering why hearing Danni call him that somehow felt really right.

He was probably just tired, Stone told himself.

Chapter Seven

Stone was back downstairs less than fifteen minutes later, his hair still damp and rakishly unkempt.

Returning to the kitchen, he found that the small, circular table in the nook had been set. His daughter was currently seated at one of the place settings and, miracle of miracles, she remained still.

Well, still for Ginny, he mentally amended.

"Daddy!" Her small face lit up when she saw him. "Now can we start?" she asked not him, the way he would have expected, but the woman setting out three small, perfect, golden-crusted potpies. No doubt prepared from scratch, they still had heat, not to mention tempting aroma, wafting from them.

"Well, that was a first," Stone murmured, sitting down on one side of his daughter.

"You don't take showers?" Danni asked.

"I don't take showers in other people's homes," he specified. "Especially not other people's homes that I'm working on."

After she finished putting out what she and Ginny had made for this rather late lunch, Danni sat down on the other side of Ginny—which also happened to be right next to Stone.

She liked his slightly messy and curly hair like that. It made him look more boyish and not quite so serious.

"You know, you could have taken longer," Danni told him. "Ginny and I would have still waited for you."

Stone realized that she was looking at his hair as she spoke. Probably thought he should have dried it before coming down, he guessed. There was a hair dryer plugged in just next to the sink, but he didn't feel quite right about using it. It was bad enough he'd had to use her towel to dry himself off. He couldn't get over feeling as if he was imposing.

"The shower was long enough," he told her matter-of-factly. And then he transformed into her contractor instead of a guest at her table. "I did hear some clanging coming from the pipes when I ran the hot water," he mentioned.

By the expression on Danni's face, he guessed he wasn't telling her anything new.

"I forgot to mention that the other day. It does that every time I take a shower or use the hot water in my bathroom. If I run cold water—" she waved her hand in the air "—nothing."

He nodded. What she'd just described wasn't that rare a problem. "I'll look into it when I'm remodeling the master bath," he promised. "Most likely, the pipe just needs to be bracketed down better."

As he talked, Stone sank his fork into the potpie on his plate and took his first tentative bite, his mind still on the noisy pipe.

The moment his taste buds kicked in and stood at attention, his mind did an instant about-face. Surprised, Stone looked down at the meal before him. The potpie was still rather hot, but that wasn't what had captured his attention. He was far from a discerning food critic with a delicate palette, but he wasn't one of those people who just ate to live, either. And even if he had been, the first bite he'd taken registered with quiet fanfare.

"This is good," he told her, making no effort to hide his surprise.

A smile played on her lips in response. "You were expecting to be poisoned?" Danni asked him, amused.

Stone raised his eyes and they held hers for a moment as he weighed his answer.

"Honestly?" he asked her.

Okay, this can't be good, not if he says it that way. Danni braced herself for what she thought *had* to be a strange answer. "Yes."

"I was actually expecting not to have any feelings about the food one way or another," he told her. Stone could see by her expression that Danni just couldn't relate to that sort of indifference when it came to food. "For the most part, food's pretty much just fuel to me. The decent kind of food I'll finish without noticing. The bad kind I'll notice and stop eating." He nodded at the potpie as he took another hefty forkful. "But this is *really* good."

Danni smiled broadly, more than a little relieved that she had managed to make something he enjoyed eating. "Thank you."

"No, *really* good," he emphasized with gusto, as surprised as she was that he was making this admission. "Which is unusual, seeing as how it's meant to be a soupy kind of thing and I don't really like soup."

"It's not soupy," Danni protested with a laugh. "This is what potpie is *supposed* to be like." She thought for a second, then felt she'd found the perfect analogy for this he-man type. "Just think of it as stew with a crust," she suggested.

Stone considered the description. "Not bad," he told her, nodding.

Danni cocked her head. "The description, or the pie?" she asked.

When she tilted her head like that, it made him want to sink his hands into her hair, frame her face and then discover what her lips tasted like.

"Both," he answered without pausing to think about it.

"Good, because I made a couple for you to take home with you—for you, Virginia and my young assistant here," Danni added, looking over toward Ginny and drawing the little girl into her inner circle.

For her part, Stone noticed, his daughter was far too busy eating to interrupt or insert her two cents into the conversation. Whatever secret ingredient the woman had put into the pie, it appeared to have a subduing effect on his daughter.

He could really get used to that.

"Just what's in this thing?" He nodded toward the almost-consumed potpie before him.

She thought of what she'd put in. "Diced chicken breasts, peas, carrots, corn, green beans, some broth mixed with flour, pepper, salt and a little parmesan cheese—why?"

That sounded almost painfully ordinary. There had to be something more. "What else?"

She didn't quite understand what he was trying to get her to say. She could only work with what she knew: the truth as it existed in this case.

"Nothing. It's all poured into a pie crust and covered with another crust, then baked."

He still found it hard to believe—not that the ingredients she'd just quoted had turned into an exceptionally tasty meal. The woman seemed to have a tight lock on the ability to make almost anything taste mouthwatering. What he found almost impossible to believe was that there wasn't something "extra" done to it before she put the potpies into the oven.

"What else did you think was in there?" she asked, curious to hear his answer.

"Oh, I don't know," he said and followed it up with pure speculation. "Extract of valerian root, a dose of tryptophan, something like that."

She looked at him, a little confused. Did he think she was trying to knock his daughter out, send her to slumber land until he was finished working? Just what sort of a person did he think she was?

"Why would I use something like that? This is supposed to be a potpie, not a sleeping aid."

"I wasn't thinking of sleeping, I was thinking more along the lines of tranquilizing," he corrected, subtly indicating his daughter with his eyes. "The last time I saw Ginny that still, she had a hundred and three fever and an upper-respiratory infection. Come to think of it, Virginia fed her chicken soup then."

"Chicken soup's supposed to have some medicinal properties," she told him. "But otherwise—the similarities in behavior are purely coincidental—maybe she just responds to good food." She smiled fondly at Ginny, watching her eat her potpie as if there would be nothing in the refrigerator for her to eat tomorrow. "She likes the epicurean experience."

"What's epi—epi—that word you just used," Ginny finally said in subdued frustration. "What's it mean?" she asked.

"It means that while you're eating, you focus on just that experience and nothing else," Danni explained to the little girl. "It also means that you know good food when you sample it," she concluded affectionately, giving the wiggling little girl a quick hug before releasing her again.

Ginny's eyes sparkled. "Yeah!" she responded with feeling. "And that was *real* good."

Danni noticed with pleasure that both father and daughter had done more than justice to their meals. All that remained were empty, miniature-size pie tins.

"Who's ready for dessert?" Danni asked, pretending to look around for takers.

"I am!" Ginny declared, raising her hand and waving it above her head just in case Danni hadn't noticed it.

"Well, by golly, it certainly does look like you are," Danni commented to the little girl, then stole a glance in Stone's direction. The man hadn't left behind so much as a crumb.

At least none that could be seen.

It gave her a warm glow inside. Seeing someone enjoy one of the meals she'd prepared always did that, and this time, even more so.

"But you're not," Stone pointed out, looking at the pie tin on her plate. "You didn't finish your meal. Something we should know about?"

The second he asked, he realized that it sounded as if he was teasing her. Something he hadn't engaged in since Eva had left his life.

Maybe there *was* something in the pie, he thought, something that took down his guard, or if not took down then definitely soften.

"Only that I'm a habitually slow eater, especially when I have guests," Danni said by way of a confession. "I get too caught up in watching their reaction to the meal I made to remember to eat it myself."

Danni rose from the small, circular table, taking both of their dishes, and putting them neatly down into the kitchen sink. She then took her plate and left it on the counter. She still had more than half the potpie left to eat.

"I'll have this for dinner later," she told him.

That done, she took the chocolate pecan pie from the

back of the stove where it was cooling and brought it to the table. She placed it in the middle, then got three dessert plates, which she distributed, placing one at each place setting, before she went to get a knife.

"I believe this is the first pecan pie your daughter's ever made," she told Stone, then asked for verification of her facts, not from him but from Ginny. "Am I right, Ginny?"

The little girl bobbed her head up and down vigorously, her curls flying to and fro about her face. "Uh-huh. The first. I never baked-ed a pie before today," she said with pride.

"Well, you did such a good job, I would have never guessed," Danni told her. "It just looks delicious. Don't you think so?" she asked, turning to Stone for back-up.

Danni knew firsthand how much a father's praise meant to a daughter. She still missed hearing her own father's enthusiastic encouragement.

Her father had been supportive of her right from the start, giving her heartfelt compliments even in the beginning, when her efforts were a great deal less than stellar. Sam Everett always made a point of telling her how much he enjoyed what she made, even when she had trouble choking it down herself.

It definitely made her want to do better next time. Made her want to be worthy of the praise her father gave her.

Even though she finally found her niche and hit a high plateau, she still strove very hard to do better "next time."

"Delicious," Stone echoed, nodding his head and looking right at Ginny.

Ginny looked as if she were bursting with pride. "I'll cut you a piece, Daddy, so you can taste it," Ginny volunteered. She started to reach for the knife Danni had set down.

Rather than chide her or pull the knife away before she could get it, Danni went with what she felt was an ego-saving approach.

"Oh, you've worked hard enough today," she told Ginny, deftly putting her hand over the knife before Ginny could wrap her fingers around it. "Why don't you let me serve *you* a piece?" she offered.

With that, Danni cut a healthy-sized sliver of pie and placed it on Ginny's plate, then cut a slightly wider piece and served it to Ginny's father.

A third sliver, more the size of what she'd just given Ginny, found its way to her plate.

Since both father and daughter were waiting on her, Danni proclaimed, "Okay, people, dig in." And three forks almost simultaneously sank into their own individual mound of pecans, brown sugar, two kinds of corn syrup and a few things Danni liked to refer to as her "secret" ingredients.

From beneath hooded eyes, Danni watched her guests' reaction to her latest version of crushed chocolate pecan pie.

While she was fairly confident that they would enjoy what they were eating, that wasn't why she was watching them. She just never tired of the look of pleasure that passed over people's faces when they first sampled something that she had made. It was like receiving a merit reward for a job well done and she was the first to admit—without shame—that she thrived on that sort of feedback. For her, it wasn't rooted in insecurity. The reason she liked it was because she had a desire for affirmation and reinforcement.

"Didn't Ginny do an absolutely outstanding job?" Danni asked the girl's father.

He didn't answer immediately. Instead, he looked at her for a long moment, then slanted a glance toward his daughter. Ginny was beaming from ear to ear, obviously pleased with herself and pleased with what she was eating. Moreover, from the look of it, his daughter was also half in love with this woman she had just met. This woman had a gift not just for cooking and baking, but for calming down overenergized little girls.

Hell of an asset to have, he couldn't help thinking, looking at Danni again.

"Yes," he said, "she did a *very* excellent job," he said, pausing briefly to glance over the woman whose house he was contracted to remodel before turning back toward his daughter.

In his estimation, Ginny looked as if she were ready to walk on air at any given moment. Thanks to Danni. The woman was extremely good with children.

"Maybe I can cook other things," Ginny said hopefully, looking at Danni as she nibbled on her lower lip, the way she always did when she was holding her breath over something.

"Maybe you can," Danni readily agreed. "The next time I'm off and your dad brings you along when he comes to work on the house, you and I can put our heads together and come up with another lunch."

Ginny watched her very thoughtfully. "Does it hurt?" she asked.

"Does what hurt?" Danni asked.

"Putting our heads together. Does it hurt? And do we have to keep them that way when we're cooking?" she asked with concern.

She could have eaten her up, Danni thought. "No, sweetie, it's just an expression. We don't really have to put our heads together. As a matter of fact, we'll probably get more done if we don't."

Ginny instantly clapped her hands together, ready to sign on. "Tomorrow?" she asked hopefully, her expressive big blue eyes dancing about.

"I'm afraid I'll be busy tomorrow—I have a job," she explained to the little girl. "But we can make arrangements for a next time," she promised. She saw Ginny's face fall a few degrees, as if she felt "next time" would never happen.

She didn't want the little girl to feel that way. She would have all the time in the world to experience disappointment. It shouldn't have to be at the age of four, she reasoned.

"Sometimes I get off early," she told Ginny, lowering her voice as if she was sharing some sort of state secret. "When I do, I'll call you and if you come over with your dad, you and I could make dinner."

Ginny turned her laser-beam eyes on her father. "Can we, Daddy? Can we?" Ginny begged.

"We'll see," he told her.

"We'll see *yes*, Daddy. We'll see *yes*," Ginny pleaded because she knew that when her father said the phrase, "we'll see," it usually meant no in the long run.

He looked at Danni then, not sure if he felt overwhelmed or just in awe of her methods.

"You were right," he told her.

Danni wasn't sure just what he was referring to. They'd found themselves on opposite sides of a few issues. "About what?"

"When you told me to bring Ginny with me because you were good with kids," he told her. "If anything, you didn't do yourself justice."

Danni laughed, more pleased than she thought she would have been to hear his praise.

"It's not a matter of being good with kids really. It's just a matter of being good with short people. That's what kids really are, you know. Just short people on their way to becoming tall people." She looked at Ginny with a warm smile. "What do you say to helping me pack up a few potpies and the rest of this chocolate pecan pie so that your dad can take it home and you two can have the rest of this later on tonight?"

Ginny needed no further convincing. Danni had had her with the phrase: "What do you say to—"

Ginny's response was a resounding "Sure!"

Stone had a feeling that if this woman with the hundred-watt smile and killer legs had asked his daughter to come slay dragons with her, she would have gotten the same response.

He wasn't doing remodeling for a celebrity chef,

Stone thought, he was remodeling the living quarters of a sorceress.

A damn *sexy* sorceress.

Which meant, among other things, that he was going to have to watch his step.

Chapter Eight

"I like her, Daddy. Do you like her?" Ginny asked some time later as they were driving home from Danni's house.

They had lingered awhile longer, after their hostess had packed up the extra potpies, along with what was left of the chocolate pecan pie, to take home with them. They had stayed predominantly to help with clean-up after the impromptu meal.

Stone had to admit that he was pretty stunned when it was Ginny, not Danni, who had come up with the suggestion to clean up.

And he was even *more* stunned when his daughter dove into said cleanup eagerly, especially since this was the child who couldn't be coaxed into cleaning her room and required excessive bribery to pick up her toys off the family room floor.

Eagerly, but slowly, he noted her pace. When he commented on her abbreviated speed, she'd looked at him with her doelike eyes and said, "If I'm too fast, then I'm not doing it well."

She had parroted back a sentiment that he had once expressed to her.

His daughter was clearly up to something.

The suspicion rose again now, with the question she'd just put to him. The one he hadn't answered yet.

"Well, do you, Daddy?" Ginny pressed.

Most of the time, when his pint-size woman-in-training asked a question, it was just sufficient for him to grunt or make some sort of noise that passed for a reply and she, in typical female fashion, just continued with her monologue. Rarely, if ever, did Ginny require an actual verbal response.

This was different.

After having asked her question, she obviously wanted some kind of input from him. Most likely, if he was any kind of judge of voice tones, Ginny was looking for him to agree with her and say that he liked the woman.

So, to bring an end to this, Stone told him daughter, "Yes, she's nice."

He hadn't expected Ginny to seize the word and all but run with it.

"Very, very nice," she declared with feeling. "I think Danni's the nicest lady I ever met."

This seemed to be getting a little out of hand, Stone thought. "Nicer than Aunt Virginia?" he asked Ginny, curious now to hear how his daughter would respond.

Ginny started to say "Yes," then stopped. He could almost hear her thinking.

"Not nicer," she finally said. "But she's just as nice as Aunt Virginia."

Well, at least Ginny's loyalty was still intact, he thought, somewhat amused. He quickly reviewed the day's events as he knew them. Granted he'd been working a good deal of the time that she had spent with Danni. Maybe something had happened when he wasn't around that had created this feeling about the woman. If so, he wanted to know just what had happened.

"Why are you so impressed with her?" Stone asked his daughter.

"'Cause," Ginny responded. No other words followed in the single word's wake. That alone was highly unusual.

The light up ahead at the major intersection was red. Stone eased to a stop behind a blue van with a dented bumper and took the opportunity to glance into the rearview mirror.

Securely strapped into her car seat, Ginny was waving her feet back and forth like a metronome set on triple time, a sure sign that she was agitated or exceedingly excited about something.

He was right. Something was definitely up with his daughter, but he hadn't a clue what it was. Whatever it was, it had something to do with Danni Everett.

Was Ginny acting like this because, in a vague sort of way, Danni bore a slight resemblance to her mother, to Eva? Did some part of Ginny remember her mother and was responding to this new woman on that level?

No, Stone decided in the next moment, he was reading far too much into this. She'd been just a baby when Eva died.

The Smartcar behind him beeped. The high-pitched sound registered just as he saw that the light had turned green and the dented van that had been in front of him was now halfway down the next street. He took his foot off the brake and pressed down on the accelerator again.

There was probably a far simpler explanation for what was going on. Ginny was probably just responding to Danni because the woman had displayed an interest in her and had had Ginny "help" her make both the main dish and the dessert.

That was something a mother might do—and something he knew that Virginia had never done with Ginny. Virginia, God bless her, was good at a lot of things, but anything that involved preparing a meal was completely out of his sister's realm of expertise. Virginia's talent for cooking began and ended with dialing the phone for takeout.

So helping in the kitchen was an entirely new experience for Ginny, one that, from the bits and pieces of dialogue he had picked up at the table, made his daughter feel quite proud of herself. There was no underestimating the value of something like that, he thought.

Consequently, Ginny was associating that feeling of well-being and pride with Danni, which was why she was so high on the woman.

So, rather than try to explore any different reasons behind Ginny's sudden and strong attachment to Danni

Everett, he opted to go along with his daughter's enthusiastic pronouncement—and hope that was the end of it.

"She *is* pretty nice, isn't she?"

He didn't think he'd ever seen Ginny beam as hard as she did this time around.

"Yes!" she agreed with even more zest. He was definitely *not* prepared for what came out of her mouth next. "Can we go back there again tomorrow? To Danni's house?"

"Well, I have to," he told her, "because I'm working on her house. But you're going to be staying home with Aunt Virginia."

He trusted that his sister's "sudden emergency" meeting with her potential new client was a one-time occurrence and that she would once again be available to stay with Ginny while he worked. All they had to get through was the summer. Once they were past that, Ginny would be in first grade and things would get a little easier.

At least he could hope.

"But what if Aunt Virginia's busy again?" Ginny asked.

Was that a hopeful note he heard in Ginny's voice? "She won't be."

"But what if she *is?*" Ginny pressed, obviously determined to get an answer out of him.

Stone sighed. Ginny wasn't about to let this go. "Then you can come with me again," he told her. Darting a quick glance into the rearview mirror again before looking back at the road, he saw Ginny elaborately crossing her fingers as she squeezed her eyes shut.

His daughter was making a wish.

This woman had *really* cast a spell over the little girl. He had never seen her behaving like this. "But if that happens, it'll be just the two of us at the house."

Another quick glance showed him that Ginny's face had fallen. "Why?"

"Because Danni will be at work. She tapes that cooking program on some cable channel," he reminded Ginny. "I don't remember the name of the show."

"Danni's Desserts to Die For," Ginny rattled off. "Then can we go there?" Ginny asked. "To watch her make things?"

Her mind was like a steel trap. Even so, he was surprised she remembered the name of the program when he didn't. This woman *had* snared his daughter's heart. Maybe he should have paid a little closer attention to her, he told himself.

In the next moment, he reminded himself that he was currently "seeing" someone, which meant he should *be* paying closer attention to another woman, not Danni.

"Number one," he told Ginny, "Danni would have to invite us to come on the set, we can't just show up. And number two, if we *did* go there, then I wouldn't be working on her house, which is what she's paying me to do, remember?"

"Oh." It was a very small, sad little sound. His daughter knew how to play him, Stone couldn't help thinking. "Then I guess you'd better work on her house, huh?"

Stone struggled to suppress a laugh. "Yes, I guess I'd better," he agreed.

"But you will see her again, right, Daddy? If you

work on her house, she'll want to see what you're doing, right?"

Stone thought that was rather an odd question to be coming from a four-year-old, even if that four-year-old *was* going on forty. For now, he set her mind at ease. "I have to," he told Ginny.

She didn't leave it at that—not that he thought she would. His assurance just opened the door for yet another question. "Will you be seeing her a lot?"

Glancing to his right, he changed lanes, preparing to turn down the next corner. "Well, she's the one who has to make the final decisions about each of the rooms I'm remodeling for her, so yes, I'll probably be touching base with Danni pretty often." He waited until he turned at the end of the next block before asking, "What's this all about, Ginny? Why are you so interested in whether or not I'll be seeing Danni?"

Ginny raised and lowered her shoulders in an exaggerated shrug. A movement Stone caught the tail end of as he looked up into the rearview mirror for a split second.

"I dunno," she told him, suddenly looking every bit the four-year-old. "I think Danni's fun," she finally said.

So she'd already said. But this time it began making sense and falling into place for him. This woman had paid real attention to his daughter and she'd played with her. As opposed to Elizabeth, who was polite to Ginny, but for the most part, she didn't really seem to be able to relate to his daughter at all.

"And you don't think that Elizabeth's fun, do you?"

he asked, even though he was pretty sure he knew the answer to that.

"Elizabeth's not fun," Ginny answered flatly. The simple statement confirmed his suspicions.

"Well, we'll see if we can change that," Stone promised. He was going to talk to Elizabeth about their including Ginny the next time the two of them went out together.

When had life gotten to be so complicated and tricky? It used to be something he'd just glide through without any effort, and now, he was constantly facing choices, with forks in the road that necessitated decisions every step he took. He missed the simple times.

He missed Eva.

Elizabeth Wells was the first woman he'd gone out with since Eva had died. One of his friends, Jeremy Banks—they started out in the general contractor business together—had introduced him to Elizabeth. She was the cousin of Jeremy's wife and, at the time he'd introduced them, Elizabeth had just stopped seeing some politician. Jeremy thought the two of them might hit it off. He and his wife had invited them both to their house for dinner.

Elizabeth, who was a press secretary for the mayor's office, was certainly attractive enough and interesting enough to warrant his asking her out. Stone knew that he felt like half a person ever since Eva had left his life and, while the work he did as well as raising Ginny certainly kept him busy, there was this empty spot inside of him that nothing seemed to fill.

So he had agreed to give dating a try.

Dating, he thought with a shake of his head. Who would have ever thought that after having what he'd considered a perfect fairytale life with a woman he adored and a baby they were both crazy about, that he would suddenly find himself back trying to navigate the dating pool?

"Okay, Daddy," Ginny said gamely, agreeing to something he'd said earlier. Stone spent thirty seconds wracking his brain, trying to remember just what it was he'd said. "I'll try to like Elizabeth."

Well, that sounded hopeful, he thought, taking her words at face value. "That's my girl."

He noticed that this time, she didn't smile the way she usually did when he called her that.

He *definitely* needed to have a talk with Elizabeth about opening up more to his daughter.

Virginia was home by the time he and Ginny arrived. Parking the car, he undid his daughter's car-seat straps and placed her on the driveway, then went to take out the leftovers his newest client had all but forced on him.

Ginny was already at the door, standing on tiptoes and ringing the doorbell. "It's us, Aunt Virginia," she declared at the top of her lungs.

The door swung open less than half a minute later. "How did it go?" she asked her brother as he crossed the threshold after Ginny. "And what is that wonderful aroma?" she asked.

"Not badly and leftovers," Stone said, heading straight for the kitchen.

It took Virginia a moment to unscramble his answers

and assign them to the right questions. By then, Stone had put the leftovers down on the table. "How did it go for you?" he asked.

"For me?" Virginia asked, momentarily bewildered at his question.

"Yes, you told me that you had an interview. With a new client. That's why you said you couldn't watch Ginny, remember?" For the first time it occurred to him that perhaps Virginia *hadn't* had an interview to see to. But if she didn't, why had she said that she had? Things just weren't adding up.

"Of course I remember," she said almost indignantly. "And it went just the way I expected it to," she told him, mentally crossing her fingers and hoping, if this all went the way it should, that her brother would find it in his heart to forgive her for bending the truth this way.

What "bending?" You're lying and you know it. But it was for a good cause, she told herself.

"You landed the client?" he asked her, taking down three dessert plates out of the cupboard.

"Like he was a salmon and I got between him and upstream," Virginia said with a pleased laugh. She was rather proud of herself for the image she'd just verbally drawn.

"So you can watch Ginny for me tonight?" he asked Virginia.

"Sure." Following her brother's lead, she took out forks and placed them next to the plates. "Are you going out?" she asked hopefully.

"Going out," he confirmed.

There was no need for either Virginia or Ginny to

know that he was going to call Elizabeth first and see if perhaps he could either coax her to come over so that they, meaning she, could spend more time with Ginny. Or to at least broach the idea to her and perhaps make arrangements to bring Ginny along with them this weekend. Maybe they could take in a movie or go to an amusement park.

"That was fast work," Virginia couldn't help commenting.

Stone looked at her, confused. "I worked at my usual pace," he told her.

Trust Stone to be too literal. "Wait," Virginia said, putting her hand up. Something didn't feel right. "You're going out with—"

"Elizabeth," he answered, wondering why she had to ask. "Who else?"

"Who else indeed," Virginia said under her breath as she watched her brother go up the stairs to change into fresh clothing.

So far, this wasn't exactly going according to plan, she couldn't help thinking.

But then, as the cliché went, tomorrow was another day.

And she prayed it would go better tomorrow.

"You're joking, aren't you?" Elizabeth asked with a touch of impatience a few minutes later as they spoke on the phone.

He was getting a bad feeling about this. No part of his conversation so far had suggested that this was going to be the comedy portion of their verbal exchange. "No, I'm being serious."

"You want to include your four-year-old on our next date," Elizabeth repeated incredulously. And then, after a rather audible sigh, she seemed to regroup. "Stone, honey, if you feel you're not seeing enough of your daughter, I understand. Really," she emphasized, making him doubt that she understood anything at all. "Spend some time with her. Take her to one of those God-awful animated movies you just mentioned. We can go out some other night," Elizabeth told him.

He couldn't help feeling that the leash about his neck was being temporarily loosened. All he could focus on, though, was that there *was* a leash.

When had *that* happened?

One of his most cherished memories was the last time he, Eva and Ginny had gone out as a family. Ginny was two and a half at the time. They had gone to a matinee at the neighborhood movie theater to see a rerelease of a famous cartoon classic. He could have sworn that Eva enjoyed it just as much as Ginny had.

It was Ginny's first experience going to the movies and her eyes had been as big as saucers for the entire movie. She'd also insisted on standing up rather than sitting down, afraid that if she was sitting, she'd somehow miss something that was on the screen. She'd been incredibly excited about what they were watching.

They'd each sat on one side of Ginny, he and Eva, and he remembered thinking that this was the way life was supposed to be, enjoying these tiny, sparkling pockets of time that were absolutely perfect.

Less than two weeks later, Eva was gone. Just like that. And he'd felt as if someone had gutted him using a jagged spoon.

He'd started seeing Elizabeth in hopes of getting rid of that feeling. But maybe, he now thought, this wasn't the way to go.

"I take it you don't like animated movies," he said to Elizabeth, exhibiting a great deal of restraint as far as he was concerned. The fact that she didn't somehow insulted the memory of Eva for him.

Stone could almost envision Elizabeth's expression, half amazement that he should even ask such a question and half pity that he had entertained the thought that she might *like* watching cartoon characters cavorting across a movie screen.

"Should I?" she asked with a touch of disdain. "They're made for children."

Stone thought of letting that pass uncontested, but then he heard himself saying, "To appeal to the child in all of us."

Elizabeth laughed in response. "Now you sound like a production marketing executive. I like movies that are intended for adults, Stone. The 'child' in me grew up a long time ago. But, like I said, if you feel you need to connect with your daughter, then by all means, do it so that you can stop feeling so guilty. We'll just go out some other time."

It was on the tip of his tongue to inform her that this had nothing to do with guilt and that part of him actually resented the off-handed assessment. He'd spent the better part of the day, in one form or another, with

Ginny, so it wasn't a matter of needing to connect. *He* wasn't the one who needed to connect with his daughter.

Better luck next time, Stone thought philosophically.

"I'll be over by eight," he told her.

"I take it that eight *is* past her bedtime?"

"Yes." He told himself he shouldn't be feeling this sudden resentment toward the woman. She'd never had children of her own and this was a learning process for her.

But Danni didn't have any kids, either, a voice in his head said. *And she related to Ginny just fine.*

He shut the voice out.

"Wonderful," Elizabeth was saying with a note of triumph—as if she'd just thrown the dice and come up a winner. "I'll be here, waiting."

For some reason, Stone felt as if he'd just been put on notice.

Chapter Nine

"I have no kitchen," Danni cried as she walked into what had been, up until just now, the center of her home. She'd arrived from the studio early and had walked through the house, looking for Stone and curious as to his progress. The noise of groaning plasterboard under attack had led her to the back of the house.

Once on the scene, it took Danni a couple of moments to recover.

They were three weeks into renovating the forty-plus-year-old house and so far, she had dealt with looking at stripped walls and exposed, ugly pipes in all three of her bathrooms and had put up with a family room that looked as if a bomb had gone off in the middle of it.

But seeing her kitchen devoid of everything that made it a kitchen in the first place—the stove, the refrigerator, *both* sinks, everything, included the overhead light panels and the walls—well, it made her feel as if her very identity had been diced, sautéed and then thrown down the garbage disposal to be ripped into tiny bits.

Danni had deliberately come home early—having moved up her program's taping schedule for the day—so that she could touch base with her general contractor and discuss mundane things like where to shop for rugs and stone flooring. These areas, she was clueless about. Her life had always been filled with far too many details for her to take note of the best places that catered to home rejuvenation.

She hadn't expected to be jarred by the sight of a war-zone kitchen.

Surprised—she hadn't said anything about arriving home while he was still here, working—Stone dropped the crowbar he'd been using to pry away the discolored, cracked tile from the counter beside the gaping hole that had once been the double sink.

Recovering, Stone laughed at her exclamation. "For my sister, that would be a reason to rejoice and an excuse to go nuts, ordering takeout," he told her. For the first time, he took in Danni's shell-shocked expression. "But I guess not for you," he speculated.

What she was looking at took her breath away—and not in a good way. Even the floor—he'd removed the dark brown vinyl with its embossed, cracked octagon design—felt uneven beneath her feet. Splotches of dried glue yet to be pried off added to the unevenness.

Doing anything in this shell of a room before Stone got around to remodeling it would be immensely challenging, Danni thought, already trying to deal with the challenge. She couldn't conceive of not having some sort of a kitchen to work in.

"I guess I could put up a card table and have a hot plate on it." And then a thought hit her and she looked around at what was left of the walls—or where the walls had been this morning when she'd left for the studio. "I do still have sockets so I can plug in a hot plate and a coffeemaker, right?"

"One," he told her, pointing to the opposite wall. He hadn't gotten around to removing it yet so that he could check the wiring, making certain that it was sound.

Danni smiled as she nodded. "One's all I need to plug in the coffee in the morning and a hot plate to cook on at night."

The woman had to be one of the most exceedingly flexible people he'd ever met. He liked the way she was able to adjust to any circumstances. He'd certainly dealt with enough home owners to be impressed with Danni's low-key attitude. She hadn't gone off the deep end when she saw that her creative center had been demolished. That spoke well of her resilience.

"Like your morning coffee, eh?" he asked, amused. That gave them something in common. He couldn't fully function without his.

"My eyes don't officially open until the second cup," Danni willingly admitted.

Stone laughed, nodding his head. "Me, too," he told her. "I'm dead asleep until I've consumed my second cup of what I'm told passes as a giant cup of double espresso. My sister threatens to run a coffee IV through my arm so I sound human first thing in the morning instead of like—her word," he quoted, "Bigfoot."

As Danni listened to him, she looked around again, thinking she might have acclimated to what she saw. But the view was as abysmal the second time around as it had been the first. Maybe even a touch more, since there were gaping holes, which she now noticed.

She didn't want him to think she was trying to rush him in any way, but she needed something to hold on to and schedule around.

"Just how long does it have to stay like this?" she asked, doing her best to sound as if she were just curious and fighting off a full-blown panic attack. She didn't want him to think she was a flake, but she *did* need her kitchen.

Squatting down, he tucked the crowbar away into the larger of the two tool bags he'd brought into the house today.

That done, he rose again, looking into her eyes and thinking how incredibly blue they were before saying, "That depends."

Had she made a mistake in going with this man? She'd trusted Maizie's recommendation, but maybe Maizie hadn't actually been able to have him checked out, maybe *she* was going by someone else's recommendation. Someone who had something to gain from this man getting work. Now that he'd denuded her kitchen, was he going to hold it for ransom, stretch out the project as long as possible? She wasn't paying him per diem, but maybe he would begin hinting at "incentives" for finishing faster. Incentives in this case always translated into money.

"On?" she asked, holding her breath and waiting for him to lower the boom.

"On how long it takes you to pick up the kind of stone you want for your floors, whether you want tile or granite for your kitchen counter—both, by the way, come in an array of styles, colors and shapes so there's a lot to choose from. And then there are the appliances—you get to pick out the brands, the types, the colors, well, you get the picture. The upshot is it can take anywhere from three weeks to six—not to mention that there's also the delivery to factor in."

"The delivery to factor in?" she repeated, feeling utterly lost.

Stone nodded, then explained it as simply as he could. She looked a little stunned and he felt rather sorry for her—though for the life of him, he didn't know why. He'd been in this business for a number of years now, working pretty steadily, thank God, and he'd never really identified with the home owner before. He had no idea why he did this time, but something about the woman got to him and he couldn't even begin to guess why or how this had come about.

He supposed that Ginny was to blame if anyone was. If she hadn't asked him that first day if he liked Danni, hadn't pressed him for an answer while proclaiming that *she* liked the woman, maybe this thought about being attracted to her wouldn't be rattling around in his head.

"Some things are shipped from back East," he told her. "Others might have to come from somewhere in

Europe, depending on what you finally pick out." Stone saw the rather dazed expression on her face intensifying, as if she didn't know where to begin. There was no denying that she looked rather appealing like that, like a girl—not a woman—who had suddenly realized that she'd lost her way and was in way over her head.

"Overwhelmed?" he asked, managing to successfully hide his amusement.

You have no idea, Danni thought in response.

But there was no way she was going to admit that. At least, not to the extent that she felt it. Danni had made it a point never to let anyone know if she felt outnumbered, outflanked or unequal to a task.

For the last three years, since her father had died, although she made friends as easily as some people breathed, at bottom she felt alone, without anyone to turn to or depend on but herself.

Oh, there'd been a brief period when she'd thought she was in love, around the time of her father's passing, but she'd discovered that Bill had seen a great deal of potential in her and had gone out of his way to hitch his wagon to her star.

His intention, she'd discovered, was to get a free ride. Exchanging compliments for cash.

When she'd found out that his bottom line involved money, not love, she'd quickly sent him packing. So now she was her own person, no matter how lonely that turned out to be at times.

"Stone," she confessed, "I don't have the first clue where to go to find any of this stuff or how to go about finding out."

He *knew* she was going to say that, he could feel it in his bones. Lucky for her, he had the solution to her dilemma.

"No problem. I can give you addresses to different stores—there're a whole cluster of stores that deal with floor, wall and counter coverings on Katella Ave, in Anaheim. They've got tile, stone, carpets, tubs, showers, more fixtures than you'd think possible—"

She held her hand up, already overwhelmed by what he was telling her and the images his words were creating in her head.

"That's what I'm afraid of. I'm going to be like Alice in Wonderland, trying to find her way home while some saleswoman besotted with the latest color in rugs yells, 'Off with her head!' in the background."

"You don't *like* shopping?" he asked incredulously. He thought all women were born loving to shop. Even Ginny enjoyed going to the mall at her tender age.

"I like 'browsing,'" Danni emphasized. "This isn't browsing, this is 'make up your mind quick or your kitchen stays naked' shopping. I don't like shopping under pressure," she admitted. "And there's the other problem, I don't have all that much time to devote to it, which means I'm probably going to wind up settling." And that didn't even take into account the problem of possibly being taken advantage of.

Stone thought for a moment, weighing the pros and cons of what he was about to suggest. The pro would be that he'd be helping a client, not to mention that there was the added bonus of spending time with an attractive woman who got more attractive each time he saw her.

He had a feeling she wouldn't even mind if he brought Ginny along. Each evening when he came home, he was subjected to his daughter's youthful version of the Spanish Inquisition, asking him if he'd seen Danni that day. When he said no, she was disappointed. If he said yes, the questions became more involved. Three weeks into this renovation project and Ginny still hadn't lost her any of her enthusiasm for the woman. Not to mention that he'd be offering his expertise and guidance to someone who seemed to be badly in need of it. This was an area where he was pretty much of an expert. That was rather heady stuff on its own.

The con was…well, he'd be giving up his Saturday, not much of a con in the scheme of things, he supposed. Except that he had a feeling Elizabeth wouldn't be happy about his working on a Saturday. It *did* cut into their time together and she really wouldn't appreciate the fact that the person he was helping was neither a senior citizen nor someone whose face could make a clock stop— except, perhaps to stare in abject admiration.

But then, things between Elizabeth and him had been rather tense these last few weeks, ever since he'd suggested bringing Ginny along on one of their dates. Each time he tried to broach the idea to her, Elizabeth would blatantly change the subject.

While they still continued to see one another, he was beginning to feel that their relationship was facing an expiration date and that date was approaching a wee bit faster than Elizabeth was happy about.

Maybe things would work themselves out and if they

didn't, well, maybe they weren't meant to. But he felt he shouldn't waste time reflecting over it.

He made up his mind and proceeded full speed ahead. "Would you like some help with selecting some of the things you need for the renovations?"

At this point, she was opened to *any* suggestions. "You mean like a crib sheet or a book to help navigate me through the wonderful world of renovations?"

Maybe she didn't want him butting in, he thought. Some people thought of this as a very private process, wanting the house to reflect their taste and no one else's.

"Well, I don't have a crib sheet or a book like that," he told her, "but I'm pretty good at making recommendations if I see the material firsthand."

She wasn't sure where he was going with this. For the most part, after their initial meeting, he'd been working on his own here, which was why she'd decided to touch base with him. But so far, he'd only been tearing things down, not building them up.

"Are you offering to buy the materials for me?" Danni asked.

Maybe he needed to spell this out for her. "I'm offering to take you to the stores and give you the benefit of my experience."

A rush of pure relief washed over her. Suppressing a squeal of joy, Danni threw her arms around his neck and cried, "Offer accepted!" with such enthusiasm, Stone started to laugh.

The sound, since she'd thrown her arms around him to express her relief and thanks via an impromptu, warm hug, seemed to rumble right through her. Rumble through her in such a way that it felt almost seductive and exceedingly sensual.

It was then that she realized just how close her face was to his.

How close her mouth was to his.

And then, as an unknown, unforeseeable force suddenly seemed to grip her, her mouth wasn't close to his anymore. It was now occupying the same exact space, the same exact coordinates as his.

One second, there was laughter, the next, that laughter had given way to silence.

And passion.

Unexpected passion.

An entire moment packed so solidly with passion that there wasn't room for anything else.

Certainly not any common sense.

But the next moment, common sense returned, moving back in and making a valiant attempt to regain control of the situation, as well as of the two participants in that situation.

As with everything else that transpired in her life, Danni took full blame for what happened. It never occurred to her to do otherwise, to blame someone else for causing this lapse in control. She was at fault.

"I'm sorry," she all but whispered, not knowing exactly where to look, yet unable to tear her eyes away from his. "I didn't mean to do that."

"Understood," he replied, trying to regain his own composure.

In his case, it involved discovering that his insides were utterly scrambled. He might have not been the person to initiate the kiss between them but he had certainly been a willing participant the second he realized what was happening.

Moreover, he hadn't been plagued by pesky rules of decorum, or even remotely entertained the thought that this shouldn't be happening, or that he was being disloyal to Elizabeth, or even—laughingly—that his client was forcing herself on him because she'd misinterpreted his signals.

For the life of him, Stone had no idea what sort of signals he gave off. But he did know one thing for certain—Danni Everett had a sweet, sweet mouth and she was one hell of a kisser.

So much so that he was more than willing to go through the whole process again.

And again.

Danni dragged in a shaky breath, not bothering to pretend that she was unaffected by what had just taken place here. "I guess you won't be accompanying me to any of the stores this Saturday."

He looked at her for a long moment. "Was it that bad?" he finally asked, then, in case she wasn't following his thought process, he elaborated, "The kiss, was it that bad?"

Her mouth dropped open as she stared at him. How had he come to that conclusion?

"No. No," she sputtered loudly. "It was wonderful." The word echoed back to her and she could feel her cheeks beginning to burn. "I mean—I just thought that you wouldn't want to go with me after I just…well, because I just…"

The woman seemed to be drowning right before his eyes. Taking pity on Danni, Stone decided to come to her rescue. "Expressed your relief and gratitude with a friendly kiss?" he suggested.

Again she could only stare at him. "You consider that a *friendly* kiss?" she asked incredulously. If that was just friendly, then what did this man consider to be a torrid kiss?

"Well, it certainly wasn't a hostile one," he told her with a wide, amused grin.

When he grinned like that, his face transformed, changing from that of a man who looked as if he were carrying the weight of the world on his shoulders and who appeared to be the very embodiment of solemnity, to one who looked more like a free-spirited boy than a man. A very handsome, sexy, appealing, free-spirited boy. "We can pretend it never happened if that makes you feel more comfortable," he said.

"It would," she admitted, wishing that it could actually be that easy. But then, if it had never happened, she wouldn't have felt—and still be feeling—that small, amazing thrill vibrating all through her.

"All right, it never happened," Stone told her with a nod of his head. He put his hand out to her, as if to seal the deal.

Danni put her hand in his and they shook on it. But deep down, that didn't change a thing.

The kiss *had* happened and she would remember it happening for a long, long while, there was no getting around that. Because that kiss, begun in innocence and sheer exuberance, had shaken the foundations of a world that she believed to be secure. Humdrum, but definitely secure.

Just went to show her that she couldn't count on anything being true these days. Not even, she thought with a deep pang, herself. And that had been her last bastion of hope, being able to count on herself, being able to know what to expect from herself.

Being able to rise to the occasion, no matter what it was.

Now she no longer knew.

"So," Stone said to her, "if you're sure you'll be available, I can swing by around ten Saturday morning, pick you up and we can hit a few of those stores, get started on the selection process."

Danni nodded numbly, belatedly realizing that she was still holding his hand. Feeling awkward, she instantly released it and dropped her hand to her side.

"Oh, would you mind if I brought Ginny along?" he asked her.

Mind? She *welcomed* it. "No sitter?" she guessed.

"Something like that." Well, now he was stuck with the story, he thought, even though he knew that Virginia would be around. "I could call around to see if I could find someone at the last minute—"

"To come with us?" she asked, not really following him.

"No, to watch Ginny." He didn't like lying and he knew he wasn't very good at it *because* he disliked it and being lied to.

"No need for that," Danni told him. "I'd love to have

Ginny along." *She'll make the perfect chaperone*, Danni thought in relief. "I've missed her enthusiasm."

"She certainly has that," Stone agreed.

And she'll have even more of that when I tell her she'd be coming along with us Saturday.

The only element interfering with this scenario was telling Elizabeth that he wouldn't be able to see her Saturday afternoon because he was going to be busy, working.

Well, technically, he was, Stone silently insisted.

He knew that wasn't going to sit well with the woman and he began to brace himself for the torrent of displeasure coming his way.

Even so, he caught himself really looking forward to Saturday.

Chapter Ten

"You're breaking *another* date with me?"

Elizabeth Wells's voice went down an octave as she came to the end of her sentence.

Rather than put off the ordeal, Stone had decided to get it over with as soon as he came home. He called Elizabeth on her cell a few minutes after he'd walked in and greeted his daughter and sister.

He could gauge Elizabeth's displeasure by whether her voice rose or fell from its normal range. If it went up an octave or so, she was annoyed, but could be persuaded to come around and make the best of it. If her voice went down, the way it did now, then she was really angry, immovable and her forgiveness wouldn't be forthcoming any time soon.

She made it sound as if he canceled dates on a regular basis. He could only recall twice, and both had been for legitimate reasons.

"It doesn't happen that often," he pointed out.

"Often enough," Elizabeth informed him coolly. "I don't like coming in third, Stone. I can handle second once in a while, but not third."

He could almost hear the icicles forming in her voice. "Third?" he questioned. He had no idea what she was talking about.

"Yes, *third*," Elizabeth emphasized. "After your work and your daughter. My job is just as demanding as yours, Stone. Probably more," she told him haughtily. "I haven't canceled on us even once."

For a moment, he lost his temper. What had started out as an exceedingly pleasant relationship with a great deal of promise had progressively become less so. The list of red flags he needed to ignore grew rather long.

He knew for a fact that Elizabeth looked down at anyone who worked with their hands, feeling intellectually superior to them. He suspected that the only reason she was still willing to see him was because he had a degree in engineering and had worked in aerospace until the industry had all but disappeared from Southern California.

His ties to the area had him reinventing himself and using his fall-back skill from when he was working his way through college: carpentry. That eventually led to his getting a general contracting license and graduating from making cabinets to building and remodeling almost anything.

Since Elizabeth worked for the mayor's office and had a degree in political science, she saw herself a cut above the people he associated with. Her attitude was getting to be a bit much to overlook.

"Did your boss ever ask you to?" he asked Elizabeth pointedly.

"What?" She snapped out the word impatiently. Elizabeth didn't like being on the receiving end of questions that challenged her statements.

"Did your boss ever ask you to cancel your plans for the evening and work on something he needed done ASAP?" Stone asked, deliberately enunciating each word so that there was no mistaking his meaning.

"That's not the point," Elizabeth informed him frostily.

"I think it is." This had all the earmarks of escalating into a full-fledged argument and he didn't want that. Taking a breath, Stone focused his efforts on calming down. After a half a beat, he tried again. "I'll make it up to you, Elizabeth."

"Don't bother," she snapped just before she slammed down the phone.

Stone stared at the phone receiver in his hand for a long moment, debating whether or not to call Elizabeth back and find some way to smooth the woman's ruffled feathers.

But then he wondered if he really *wanted* to make amends.

In the beginning, in addition to being quite attractive in a polished sort of way, Elizabeth had been bright and funny and he'd enjoyed listening to her biting wit. But, if he were being honest with himself, he never felt a hundred percent comfortable in Elizabeth's company.

A part of him sensed the woman was constantly scrutinizing him, evaluating him. It was a little like being a student in a prep school, knowing he didn't dare allow himself to slouch.

He'd never put on any airs to try to impress anyone. If anything, he *was* guilty of the sins of omission, of not saying what he knew might lead to a less than amicable conversation. He let her talk and at times let her believe that he agreed with her on some trivial matters close to her heart when he really *didn't* agree at all.

And, most important of all, even slightly more important than never feeling that he could really just be entirely himself, was the fact that Elizabeth didn't fill that emptiness within him.

That had been the whole original point for his giving in to Jeremy and going out with the woman to begin with, to try to fill that hole that Eva's passing had opened up in his gut.

"If you'd like to place a call…" the metallic, female voice was saying into his ear, accompanied by the annoying throbbing noise of a phone left too long off the hook.

Stone sighed. "No, I wouldn't," he muttered under his breath just before he returned the landline receiver back to its cradle.

As if guarding a major secret, Ginny stepped into the family room. She grinned from ear to ear and hugged herself gleefully.

Virginia looked up from her book.

"What's up, munchkin?" she asked, curious as to why

her niece seemed to be embracing herself while that wide grin of hers all but split her face in two. "Daddy and Elizabeth just had a fight," she announced happily.

The book about someone else's romance instantly ceased to be of interest to her, not when real life was unfolding something far more interesting before her. Virginia tossed the paperback on the coffee table.

"How do you know?" she asked.

"I heard him on the phone," Ginny told her, then, bobbing her head, she added, "I heard her, too."

"He had it on speaker phone?" Virginia asked, wondering why Stone would do that. Her brother was very big on privacy.

But how else could Ginny have overheard what Elizabeth was saying?

Ginny shook her head. "She was using a big voice. I could hear it coming out of Daddy's other ear."

Virginia paused, taking in a breath. Doing her best not to laugh. She supposed that was probably the most colorful, succinct explanation of why Ginny could hear what that snob was saying to her brother.

Virginia knew that she shouldn't be encouraging Ginny to eavesdrop, that she should tell her it's wrong. But they could have that heart-to-heart talk some other time. Right now, her curiosity was getting the better of her and she needed answers.

"So you know what they were arguing about?"

Ginny bobbed her head up and down like a dashboard bobble-head on a road trip. "Daddy told Elizabeth he couldn't see her on Saturday because he had to do something for his work. He said he'd make it up to her, but she yelled, 'Don't bother.'" Ginny cocked her head, her small eyebrows knitting together in confusion. "What's 'making it up to her' mean?" she asked.

"Doing something nice later on because you can't do something you promised right now" was the best way Virginia knew how to explain the phrase to her niece.

It seemed to do the trick because the little girl's eyes began to sparkle as her grin bloomed again. "You know what I think, Aunt Virginia? I think Elizabeth's going to go away." Ginny was practically beside herself with excitement.

Virginia nodded her head. Certainly sounded like that to her. "Looks promising," she agreed.

"What looks promising?" Stone asked as he entered the family room. After his less than cheerful phone conversation with Elizabeth, he needed a dose of sunshine and that meant being with his daughter.

"The weather on Saturday," Virginia said quickly before Ginny had a chance to blurt out the truth. Ginny was sharp enough, even at four, to play along.

"The weather here's always promising," he said, wondering why his sister would even think to say that. "You have plans?" he asked.

"Nothing special," Virginia answered with a vague shrug. She remembered that she was supposed to be watching Ginny because Stone had told her he was seeing Elizabeth on Saturday so she used that scenario to build on. "Just taking Ginny to the park for a while maybe. I haven't really decided yet."

"Well, you don't have to make any decisions," he told her. "You're getting the day off." He saw the quizzical look on Virginia's face and explained, "Ginny and I are going to pick out tile." Realizing that this was coming as a surprise to Ginny, Stone looked at his daughter. "I know it's boring, kiddo, but—"

He got no further as Ginny clapped her hands together as if she'd just been told she was going to live in Sleeping Beauty's castle.

"I love tile, Daddy!" she declared with gusto, fairly jumping up and down.

Stone could only stare at her. He knew she liked Danni, but he hadn't even told her that part yet. Had she just assumed they were shopping with Danni? Otherwise, this made no sense. "Since when?"

"Since I was a little girl, Daddy. A long time ago," she answered with a toss of her head.

Stone pressed his lips together, doing his damnedest not to laugh. "My mistake. I forgot," he solemnly "apologized." "By the way, Danni's coming with us. It's her tile we're going to be picking out."

Virginia rose from the sofa, more pleased than she could possibly put into words. "Looks like things are going well for you and Danni."

"The renovations are coming along, yeah," Stone agreed, deliberately avoiding assigning any other meaning to his sister's words. There was no *and* between Danni and him. They weren't a couple, a unit. They weren't *anything*.

You sure about that? She'd been on your mind a lot for someone who wasn't "anything," a small, annoying voice in his head insisted on pointing out.

Because she knew that no one could talk Stone into

anything or force him to do anything, Virginia let his answer ride for the time being. There was time enough to work on it—and him—later. Right now, all that mattered was that he was seeing Danni on Saturday and he *wasn't* seeing Elizabeth on that day.

"I'd better go see about dinner," she told him, then paused in the doorway, waiting for instructions. "Chinese or Italian?" she posed.

"Italian," he responded without thinking.

"Pizza it is," Virginia said as she went to place the order to the near-by restaurant that was on their speed dial.

Stone could have sworn he heard his sister singing, "Ding-dong, the witch is dead," under her breath and wondered what had come over her.

He also knew that there would be no finding out, no questions properly answered. Virginia could be very elusive when she wanted to be.

The older he got, he decided, the more mysterious women—all women—became. He resigned himself to the fact that trying to understand them was a losing battle and always would be.

"But, Barry," Danni lamented, "it's Saturday."

"I know it's Saturday, babe. I've got this handy-dandy thing on my desk called a calendar so I can tell people like you I know what day of the week it is." And then her producer's voice grew serious. "You think I'm happy about this? Saturday's the only day of the week I get to sleep in. Sally drags my butt to early mass every single Sunday. Like seeing me there, nodding off in the pew is going to change any plan He's got in store for me," he commented. "But the powers that be need this one segment of the show retaped," he stressed. "You gotta come in."

Barry reverted to his standard coaxing tone, the one he used dealing with studio heads and actors alike.

"Look, sweetheart, it'll only take an hour. Ninety minutes, tops. Then you can go do whatever it is you were going to do. At least you're only putting a little of your day on hold. I can't just go home and pretend nothing happened so I can get back to sleeping in once we're done," the man complained. He assumed that he'd convinced her and asked, "How soon can you get here?"

Danni heard her doorbell ringing.

They were here.

What was she going to tell them? she wondered, disappointment washing over her. She was looking forward to this on so many levels, not the least of which was finally picking out some of the things to keep the renovations moving along.

"Soon," she promised.

"Okay. Oh and don't forget to wear what you were wearing yesterday so there's continuity. Your viewers won't understand why you did a sudden costume change in the middle of making those cake pops."

"Fine. Same clothes," she parroted. "See you then," Danni said, quickly terminating the call just as she opened the door to Stone and his daughter.

The second she did, Ginny erupted like a happy firecracker.

"Hi!" she exclaimed with exuberance as she bounced

into the house. "Daddy said you need help picking out tile."

"Hi, yourself," Danni said, greeting the little girl. The grin on Ginny's face was infectious. Danni could feel it spreading to her lips even as she turned toward Stone to make her apologies and explanations.

But then she got an idea.

"There's been a slight change in plans," she started to explain, nodding at the phone in her hand. "My producer just called."

"You have to go in," Stone guessed.

She nodded her head, but before she could say anything, he was absolving her of any guilt she might be feeling. What he was feeling, oddly enough, was a sense of disappointment. He tried to pinpoint exactly why that was, even as he deliberately nixed that it could be because of Danni.

"Hey, I understand," he told her. "We can do this some other time."

"No," Ginny cried.

Danni took one look at the disappointed expression on Ginny's face and did a quick recalculation, going with the idea that had just popped into her head.

"No," she said, echoing Ginny's protest and accompanying it with a firm nod of her head.

Now he was really confused. "No?" Stone asked, looking for enlightenment.

"No, we don't have to do this some other time," she told him. "We really need to get started today." She was really tired of looking at naked, stripped-down walls when she came home at night.

He wasn't the one who had just said she had to go into the studio this morning. *She* had. "But you just said—"

Danni stopped him right there. They were wasting precious time. Every moment they stood here, talking was another moment that freeway traffic to the studio wound up doubling. They had to get going now if they wanted to have a prayer of getting to the studio at a relatively decent time.

She stopped to find her purse. "I know what I said and I do have to go to the studio, but how would you like to come with me?" She was addressing her words to Ginny. "You can sit in the studio audience—you can *be* my studio audience," she told her. "And once we get this one scene redone, we can go look at tile. Unless you'd rather not go to the studio," she said as that possibility occurred to her. Driving to Burbank and back might just be too much trouble to put Stone through.

Stone never got a chance to answer. Ginny beat him to it.

"I want to go to the studio," Ginny assured her. "Please, Daddy, can we? Can we?" she asked twice, just in case he'd missed hearing her beg the first time. Ginny grabbed his hand, all but jumping up and down, pulling on it, as if that would help persuade her father to agree.

There were very few times Stone said no when it came to his daughter. This was not one of them. Instead, he turned toward Danni.

"You don't mind?" he asked.

"Mind?" she repeated, mystified. "Why should I mind? In case you missed it, I'm the one who just suggested it. I've got people in the studio audience watching what I do every day. It might as well be people I like," she told him, then glanced down at Ginny. "The studio audience gets to sample what I make when I finish."

There, that should seal the deal for Ginny, she thought, just in case the little girl was thinking of changing her mind.

Changing her mind was the furthest thing from Ginny's mind right now. If anything, Ginny's eyes were shining. "Really?"

Danni's grin almost matched the little girl's. "Really."

Ginny swung around to make her final appeal to her father.

"Say yes, Daddy, say yes," she pleaded.

Stone responded with a deep, rumbling laugh. "As if I've ever said no to you."

"But you did say no to me, Daddy," Ginny reminded him very seriously. "I asked for a pony for Christmas and you said no. Don't you remember?"

He remembered very well. Remembered, too, feeling badly about denying the little girl *anything.* Even something as outlandish as her very own pony. There were times when he felt, if he looked up the term *pushover* in the dictionary, there would be a picture of his face in the reference area.

"That was different. I was thinking of the pony," he teased now. "And your aunt Virginia who'd be stuck cleaning up after the pony."

Ginny's small face scrunched up as if she were untangling what her father had just said.

But the bottom line was that she was really interested in one thing. "Then we can go with Danni?"

Stone nodded. "We can go."

He wasn't sure just which felt better, being on the receiving end of Ginny's hug or Danni's smile. He decided that it was a tie.

Chapter Eleven

Ginny, her hand wrapped tightly around Danni's as they walked onto the sound stage, appeared to be trying to take everything in at once.

"If your head spins any faster, it's going to fall off," Stone warned his daughter, amused as he watched her looking around.

"Is this where you work, Danni?" Ginny asked, no doubt overcome by the hugeness of it all.

"This is where I work." Danni had led the father and daughter duo in via the rear stage entrance, which brought them right to the actual set.

The set, with its gleaming new appliances, was the epitome of a state-of-the-art kitchen. It was, in a nutshell, her dream kitchen. Sometimes, after the show was done for the day, Danni would stay late to make something to take home with her or to give to one of the crew members as a gift if they happened to be celebrating some special occasion.

The crew all loved her.

Rather than behave like a diva, something that some celebrities did when they became caught up in their own press releases and started believing them, Danni never put on airs. She made it a point to know the entire staff and crew by their first names.

She also made it a point to find out about their families. Her accessibility as well as her likeability made the atmosphere on the set a great deal warmer and more laid-back than most sets.

The sound of her voice as she spoke to Ginny drew out both the producer who'd initially called her this morning and the director.

The latter looked more than anxious to get this re-taping over with and get back to his far-too-often-interrupted life.

"You came," Barry said needlessly as he came out onto the set to join her. That was when he saw Stone and Ginny for the first time. "And I see you brought reinforcements with you," he commented, looking the newcomers over rather intently.

Like most of the people on the set, he was protective of Danni.

"This is Stone Scarborough and his daughter, Ginny," Danni said, introducing them. "This is my producer, Barry McIntyre, and my director, Ryan Talbert." Each man nodded in turn. Barry gave her a questioning look and she knew that if she didn't want to walk onto a set full of speculation on Monday morning, she needed to set the record straight right now. "Stone and his daughter had just arrived at the house to take me tile hunting when you called this morning. Since you said it was only going to take up an hour—"

"Or so," Barry pointed out. "I said an hour or so."

"Actually, you said, 'Ninety minutes, tops,'" Danni quoted. "I'm planning on holding you to that because I don't think it's right to restrict Ginny for any longer than that."

Barry appeared a bit daunted as he glanced uncertainly over to his director.

Ryan sighed and nodded. All he could do was give it his best shot. "Let's get going then. We're reshooting the cake pops segment. For some reason, the tape on that didn't come out right."

She heard one of the cameramen chuckling. When she turned to look in the direction of the amused sound, she cocked her head as if to silently ask him why he was laughing.

The man wasn't shy about sharing. "My guess is that Wally probably ate that part of the tape—he's hoping you'll have to bake another batch of cake pops. I think the guy must have eaten about twenty of them. What he didn't eat, he took with him." The cameraman grinned. "Said it was for his kid but I've got a hunch his kid is never going to see them."

The gaffer they were talking about was the newest addition to their staff. He'd been there for a couple of months and was exceedingly friendly and talkative, but there was no denying that he really liked to eat. The man weighed about three hundred pounds and was already being referred to as a human vacuum cleaner—not always behind his back.

The term didn't appear to offend the man. At least, he just seemed to be able to laugh it off.

"Hey, where is the human vacuum cleaner?" another cameraman asked, looking around.

"Grady, don't call him that," Danni said.

"Ah, he doesn't care, Danni," Grady protested, waving away her protest.

"The man has feelings. Trust me, he cares," she stressed. Danni absolutely hated seeing any living thing picked on and teased, whether the act was blatant or covert.

Standing back, Stone was wordlessly taking in the exchange. He liked the fact that Danni was defending someone, thinking of the person's feelings when he wasn't even around. It gave Stone a little insight into the woman's character and her nature. He liked what he'd glimpsed in both cases.

"Okay, everyone, assume your positions," the director instructed, raising his voice.

"Where do you want us to sit?" Stone asked, addressing the question to the only person on the set who mattered to him besides his daughter.

"You can be the audience," Ryan told them, cutting in to answer before Danni had a chance to say a word. He pointed toward the small audience section. "Gemma, Roy, take seats in the second row. Let— Stone is it?" he asked, looking at the general contractor. Stone nodded. "Let Stone and the little princess here sit in the first row," he instructed.

Ginny giggled. "I'm not a princess," she protested—but not too strenuously.

"I don't want to bump anyone," Stone told the director.

"Don't worry about that. We couldn't get an audience back for the shoot on such short notice so we just gathered up friends and family members to serve as an audience. Audience at home is watching Danni, not memorizing who's in our studio audience and who went home. Since Danni brought you two with her, I figure she wants you to be up close and personal with the action—right, Danni?" Ryan asked, turning a weary, thousand-watt smile on his star for ten seconds.

"Whatever you say, Ryan," Danni responded, not wanting Stone to think she was making a big deal out of any of this—even though, now that she thought of it, she rather liked the idea of having the man and his daughter here, taking in what she did for a living.

By no means did she think of herself as a celebrity, but there were people who were impressed with *anyone* whose face wound up on the TV screen. She had a feeling Ginny might fall into that category—for the time being.

Danni pretended to be busy and not watch where Stone and his daughter finally wound up taking their seats, but she was acutely aware of where they sat down.

As far as she was concerned, they *were* her audience. She directed most of her words to that section of the seats—which turned out to be front and center.

"Okay, Danni, do what you do best. Action," Ryan declared.

Danni began talking to her audience in her laid-back, easy cadence. Traces of her Georgia accent wove their way through her sentences as she instructed the audience, both in the studio and at home, how to go about making one of the newest dessert fads to capture the public's fancy: elaborately decorated cake pops.

Just as she began, a heavyset man maneuvered his rather large frame into the seat next to Stone. "Made it," he sighed contentedly, more to himself than to anyone around him.

Then, as if he suddenly realized that he wasn't in the audience alone, he turned toward Stone and murmured, "I got stuck in traffic. Was afraid I was going to miss this."

This had to be that Wally character the others had talked about, Stone thought. The man's sentence was obviously begging for a reply. After a beat, Stone gave in and asked, "You enjoy watching her bake?"

"Mouth starts to water just thinking about it," Wally confessed. "The stuff she burns tastes better than what some people spend hours preparing—not that she ever burns anything," he added hastily, looking suddenly nervous, as if he realized he'd said too much. "You're not a blogger or anything, are you?" he asked.

"I'm her general contractor," Stone said to put the man at ease.

Wally immediately relaxed. "Yeah, she said something about having her house worked on. She's a real nice lady," he told Stone in a pseudo whisper. "Don't come any nicer. Knows the names and ages of my kids. And not just mine. Can't see why someone like that doesn't have a family of her own," he said with a shake of his head.

"Not always that easy," Stone commented.

Wally nodded his head in firm agreement. "No, I guess not. But she should." He took in a deep breath. The first batch of cake pops had gone into the oven and were already creating a tempting aroma. "Smell that?" he asked Stone. "That's pure talent. If I was married to a woman like that, I'd be fat," he speculated. Then as if he had a sudden reality check, Wally laughed and patted his large girth. "Or fatter," he amended with a wide grin.

The taping abruptly halted as Ryan cried, "Cut."

"Are we done already?" Danni asked hopefully. She glanced over toward the producer who was standing in the wings. The man had actually underestimated the time on this, she thought happily, glad she'd suggested having Stone bring his daughter and be part of her audience.

"No, and we won't be done unless the running commentary coming from the audience stops." Ryan glared at the late arrival.

"Sorry," Wally apologized. "Guess I got carried away with a surge of enthusiasm," he said, then raised his voice to promise, "Won't happen again."

"It does and today's desserts are going to go home with everyone *but* you," the director warned, obviously knowing that was the most effective threat he could issue to the gaffer.

Ryan's back was to Danni, so consequently he didn't see her looking at the wide staff member and he didn't see the wink she sent the man. A wink that silently assured him of his fair share of the loot as long as he played by the rules.

Taping resumed as Wally made a conscientious effort to maintain his silence.

Stone continued observing the woman. He had to admit that he really liked what he saw—she was bright, entertaining and funny—and the tempting scent of cake pops, decorated or simply rolled in powdered sugar, just seemed to enhance everything.

Especially, he noted, for his daughter.

"Well, I was almost right," Barry said the moment that the taping finally wrapped up for the day. "It was around ninety minutes."

"Not all that close," Danni contradicted, her eyes not on her producer but on the two people she'd dragged to the studio. It was time to get going. "I'll see you Monday," she told Barry, thereby effectively ending any further conversation he might have felt compelled to engage in.

Danni stripped off her coverall apron and placed it on the counter rather than going off set to put it away herself. She was constantly being told some people were paid to keep track of her aprons. Just this once, she decided to utilize said people—she hurried off the set and down into the audience seats.

"I'm so sorry," she apologized before she even reached them.

Stone was already on his feet, waiting for her. Ginny had bounced up to hers, energy about to be unharnessed.

"For what?" Stone asked. "The taping wasn't that much longer than ninety minutes," he told her.

Maybe it *was* but he didn't want her feeling badly about it. He—and more important, Ginny—had enjoyed themselves. Ginny had already consumed two cake pops—a lion and a giraffe—and she was holding two more in her hands.

His daughter, Stone thought, looked as if she were absolutely in heaven. Wisps of yellow and black frosting dotted her wide, smiling mouth. And her eyes could double as Fourth of July sparklers.

Danni flashed Stone a grateful smile. "Thanks for being so understanding. I really didn't want to miss out on getting your help selecting the tile and granite," she confessed. Turning toward Ginny, she asked, "So, what do you think? Do you like cake pops?" The answer was more than obvious, but she wanted the little girl to feel as if her opinion counted.

"I *love* cake pops," the little girl declared.

Stone laughed, thinking of the two cake pops she'd already made such short work of. "Just what she needs, a sugar high."

"I don't use sugar, I use apple sauce, remember?" Danni reminded him. "*Natural* apple sauce," she emphasized. "That's supposed to be even better than sugar in the recipe. Most people can't tell the difference."

Natural sugar or artificial sugar, the results were still going to be pretty much the same, Stone judged.

"Still going to have to scrape her off the ceiling," Stone predicted.

"But it won't be a cathedral ceiling," Danni pointed

out, as if that made all the difference in the world. "Just a normal-size one."

"You do try to find the silver lining in things, don't you?" Stone observed, amused and maybe just a little charmed by this exuberant woman as well.

"That's the only way I know how to survive," Danni admitted. The nature of her behavior was deeply rooted in her past. "Otherwise," she admitted in a rare moment of sharing, "I think I would have been pretty much plowed under by now."

"Oh? By what?" he asked. Then, the next moment he realized how that must have sounded to her, as if he was digging into her life. "Sorry, none of my business," he told her, raising his hands in symbolic surrender. "Didn't mean to pry."

She ignored his words of apology and the fact that he was backing away from the subject altogether. Granted she didn't owe him any explanations, but even so, maybe she owed herself a small twist of the release valve. She'd been carrying things around, bottled up inside her, for too long.

Danni made a conscious decision to share, telling herself that sometimes it was good to give voice to the things that weighed so heavily on her soul.

"My dad died just as I graduated college. He was a dear, sweet man who through no fault of his own left me with a mountain of bills to pay in addition to having to pay off my college loan. For about a month, I felt so swamped I could hardly breathe."

"Technically, you could have walked away from the medical bills," he told her. People did it all the time, either just picking up and moving away, or declaring bankruptcy.

Danni shook her head. Not that she hadn't considered it for all of a few minutes, but she'd come to the same conclusion she still espoused now.

"Not my style. My father would have been very disappointed in me if he knew," she confided. "Although, I do have to admit that I did lean in that direction for a little while, feeling that if I had to pay the bill, the least they could have done was save my father." She laughed shortly. "But there was no 'satisfaction guaranteed' stamped on the hospital bill. Just the words, Payment Due Now. And," she added with a shrug, "they *had* tried to save my dad, but the cancer was too far along, discovered too late…"

He filled in the blank. And what it told him was that the woman he was looking at had far more integrity than anyone he'd ever dealt with.

The lights all around them on the set suddenly dimmed. The set was being shut down, she realized. "I think they're hinting we should leave," Danni told her guests.

"Don't have to tell me twice," Stone said with a short laugh. Taking his daughter's small hand in his, he placed his other one against the small of Danni's back and said, "Let's go."

She could feel the slight pressure of his hand, could feel a wave of warmth pass all along her body. Danni had no idea why, but that in turn created a feeling of well-being, of being taken care of. It wafted through her as she allowed herself to be guided off the sound stage and out into the parking lot.

Just for a second, she pretended that for once there was someone looking after her, someone for her to lean on. It was an exceedingly good feeling.

Chapter Twelve

"I had no idea there were so many different stores that just sold tile," Danni sighed as she sank into the passenger seat of Stone's truck.

For the last two hours, ever since they'd left the studio in Burbank, she, Stone and Ginny had undertaken what amounted to a pilgrimage, going from one store after another, looking at miles and miles of tiles. So far, all the stores were located along the same stretch of road in Anaheim—many of them boasting that *their* collection of tile was *the* collection.

One store had tile only imported from Italy, another had their tile shipped in from different regions in South America. Still another only carried tile that came from France. A couple of stores got their tile from places she'd never even heard of. Each store had a slightly different twist to their collection, be it color, texture, locale of origin or something as simple as sporting a slightly different glaze.

And that, Danni discovered, didn't even begin to cover the army of cleaning products designed to keep those select pieces of tile looking brand new, or, in a couple of cases, older than time. Had it not been for the company she was keeping—both Ginny *and* Stone— Danni knew she would have been more than ready to throw in the towel after the third store.

Stone, standing outside the truck and directly next to the passenger seat, sympathized with how she had to be feeling right about now.

"Unless you know exactly what you're looking for, it can be pretty overwhelming," he agreed.

Now there was an understatement, she thought. "It makes me seriously consider living in a hotel."

Having secured Ginny's straps in her car seat, Stone came around to the driver's side and got in behind the steering wheel. He put the key into the ignition, but left it there for the moment.

"You don't strike me as the transient type," he told her.

"No, living in a hotel *permanently*," Danni underscored.

Stone paused for a moment to study her a bit more closely. And then he shook his head. "Still don't see you living out of a suitcase. You like owning things," he said, surprising her with his insight. "Don't worry, this gets better."

She'd believe it when it happened. "Are you talking

as a general contractor or as someone who's been on the other side of this process?" she asked.

"Both," he answered. There wasn't even a hint of a smile on his lips. "And I do know what you're going through," he assured her. "It feels as if you'll never make the right choice—and you're afraid of settling, but even more afraid that this process will go on forever—am I close?" he asked. This time he allowed the corners of his mouth to curve.

Danni shook her head. "No, you're not 'close,' you're dead on," she told him. Either he really *had* been through this process on his own, or someone had bared their soul to him in an attempt to get him to relate. Either way, she was glad that he understood how all this made her feel.

"If it makes you feel any better, most people don't go with the first selection they see," he said. "It usually takes more than a few trips to different stores before they find something that *really* moves them and then they go with that."

She laughed at his description of the process. "If I didn't know any better, I would have said you were describing the kind of search a person undertakes looking for a soul mate," she told him.

He didn't even need to reflect on what he'd said. Because he agreed with her. "Well, it is in a way. You make a commitment to what you pick out and wind up living with that commitment for a long time. Sometimes longer than some couples remain married. So, take your time," he advised. "You want to really like what you pick out. There's no advantage in going with the first thing you see."

She couldn't help thinking he was advising her about more than just the tile or the other household decorations they would be looking at in the near future.

Rousing herself, Danni focused on the business at hand. "Except that I'd be getting my house back," she pointed out.

"But you're having the remodeling done so that you'll *like* that house, right?" he reminded her. "Otherwise, there's no point in having it remodeled in the first place." He waited for his words to sink in. And enjoyed watching the bit of color rise up on her cheeks.

Danni was force to nod—and concede. "Makes sense."

"Now then, are you up for any more stores, or would you just rather call it a day and we can do this again some other time?" he asked.

If it were just up to her, she'd definitely opt to keep going. She liked spending this time with him. Liked his company, his wit, his masculinity that was so grounded. But there wasn't just her to consider here.

"That depends," she answered. Before he could ask her on what, Danni twisted around in her seat and looked at the little girl strapped in directly behind her. "Do you feel like going to any more stores, honey, or are you tired?"

"I'm not tired," Ginny proclaimed loudly. She kicked her feet a little as if to emphasize how *not* tired she was.

"I forgot to warn you. Ginny's a self-winding kid," Stone told her. "Just when you think she's going to be winding down, she surprises you by getting all wound up again."

Despite Ginny's overenergized state, Stone appreciated Danni's concern for his daughter and putting her comfort ahead of anything that she might have personally wanted.

"Well, then it's settled," Danni told him. "If you don't mind continuing to be my guide on this safari, let's just keep going."

"You heard the lady, Daddy, let's keep going!" Ginny called out excitedly, sounding as energetic as if she'd just taken a nap instead of run up and down the aisles of six different stores.

Stone laughed. "Well, I guess then I have my marching orders," he said as he started up the truck and pulled out of the parking lot.

"You're not marching, Daddy, you're driving," Ginny pointed out, giggling at his error.

"My mistake," Stone said "humbly."

Ginny giggled louder.

After another two hours of traipsing through stores that dealt predominantly with bathroom and kitchen tiles, as well as a couple of shops that specialized in tiles made out of marble, Danni decided that the excursion needed to come to an end for now.

"No more, please," she begged as they walked out of their umpteenth store, nauseatingly called, *Rocks to Riches*. "All the tile is beginning to look alike," she protested.

"That's because a lot of them *are* alike," he explained. "Some stores tend to carry the same thing, as well as a little bit extra, hoping that 'extra' will draw you in. Anyway, I think we've sufficiently gotten your feet wet."

"Her feet aren't wet, Daddy," Ginny corrected him, looking down at Danni's shoes. "It's not raining."

Ginny had been in rare form all day, he noted, and apparently on her best behavior as well. She wasn't a child given to tantrums, but she could get a bit cranky at times when she was tired, which by all rights, after walking around for four hours through stores that didn't have a single stuffed animal between them, she should have been. It seemed to Stone as if his small keg of dynamite was trying extra hard today.

It wasn't difficult to see why.

Ginny had taken a huge shine to Danni, so much more so than she ever had to Elizabeth. Now that he thought about it, Ginny hadn't really taken to any woman except for his sister, and now Danni, since her mother died. That said a great deal about the woman he'd been driving around for the last four hours, he mused.

"Nope, you're right," he agreed. "No rain." He looked now at Danni as they reached his truck. "What do you say to grabbing some dinner and then calling it a day?"

"Why don't we just go to my house and I'll whip up something for us?" Danni suggested, addressing her words to both Stone and his daughter.

"I think you're forgetting something," Stone pointed out.

She thought for a moment and nothing came to her. "What?"

"You have no kitchen." He hadn't thought he'd have to remind her of that.

"I have a plug and a hot plate," she countered, then grinned. "Never underestimate the ingenuity of a woman with a hot plate."

Stone laughed. "I have no intention of underestimating you," he told her sincerely. He already knew how capable and determined she was. He didn't need a refresher course. "But I thought it might be a nice change of pace for you to consume something you didn't have to slave over a hot plate to make," he told her, doing his best to look serious at the end.

His thoughtfulness left her momentarily speechless. Recovering, Danni said the first thing that came to her mind. "You forget, I *like* to cook."

He could just hear his sister's voice in her head, wholeheartedly endorsing this woman.

Stick with her, Stone. This woman's a keeper.

Most likely, his sister was also anticipating being invited over for meals a lot, he guessed. That was, if she ever did get around to moving out again.

"No, I didn't forget," he told her.

When it came to this woman, he'd found that he didn't forget anything he'd learned about her. Not the way she smiled, or the way she tilted her head when she was listening to him, or the way that she pressed her lips together when she was trying to make up her mind about something.

But that wasn't the point right now—or maybe he was just trying to bury the point because he wasn't ready to face it just yet. Because admitting, even just to himself, that he was drawn to this woman on any other level than just plain old basic physical attraction, would be leaving himself opened to the possibility of pain, raw, soul-shredding pain. He'd already been through that once and barely survived. He might not survive a second time around.

"There must be some part of you that likes to be waited on," he said.

"There is," she allowed, "but you just gave up your whole Saturday for me, so I want to do something in return."

"You did," he told her. When she looked at him quizzically, he explained, "You gave Ginny a bunch of cake pops."

"I gave Ginny cake pops because she was such a good audience," Danni said, twisting around to look at the little girl and give her a wink. Ginny beamed at her in response.

"Well, fortunately, I'm driving so that means you two have to go where I take you," Stone informed her with finality. "So I suggest you settle back and enjoy the ride, Ms. Everett."

"Guess I have no choice," Danni replied, amusement playing along her lips as she turned to face front again and settled into her seat. "But I intend to make a feast for you and Ginny once I get my kitchen back."

"It's a deal," Stone told her and, God help him, he realized that he was looking forward to the informal "date" he'd just made.

His reaction to Danni both intrigued Stone and worried him. He hadn't had feelings—real, *intense* feelings—for anyone since Eva had died. For the longest time, he actually didn't believe that he *could* feel anything again. What he'd had with Elizabeth was pleasant enough and he did like her. But he had resigned himself to his low-key attraction to the mayor's chief press secretary being as good as it got for him.

After all, he'd had passion already and while it had been wonderful, it had also led him into a land of desolation once Eva was no longer part of his life. It had taken him a very long time to heal, to feel something other than despair and dread.

Had he not had Ginny to care for, Stone didn't even want to think about the path he would have wound up taking.

Feelings were exhilarating, but they came with a price and he really didn't want to pay that price a second time.

But no matter how much he reasoned with himself, it felt as if he had no choice in the matter. Deliberately sabotaging his intent to do his job and leave before Danni came home, he caught himself lingering at her house longer and longer each evening, adding finishing touches on areas already finished, just so that their paths might briefly cross.

Just so he could see her before he went home to his daughter and his life. And even perhaps, just to touch her in passing, although the last time had resulted in not just an impersonal touch but a caress. A slow, languid caress along her jawline as he looked into her eyes. It had been on a pretext of removing a stray hair from her cheek. But there'd been no hair.

Only sizzle.

Sizzle that in turn lingered as well. Lingered because

he kissed her—although he wouldn't have been able to reconstruct the logistics if his life depended on it. One second, they were talking and he was saying, "Good night," the next, for a brief, shining, wondrous moment, their lips all but fused into one another, creating, among other things, their own personal bonfire.

But the next moment, they'd separated, each diving for cover behind inane words and cardboard sentiments they both knew didn't have a lick of truth to them.

He was later getting home than he'd ever been.

The funny thing was neither Ginny nor Virginia complained about his lateness. They hadn't even said a word when he began coming home later and later.

Ginny had always complained when he left her to see Elizabeth, but this, somehow, was different for her. Most likely it had to do with the fanciful desserts Danni began sending home with him right after they'd observed her taping that Saturday.

It got to the point where his concern wouldn't stay under wraps. He felt the need to share it with Ernie Walsh, the retired construction worker, now part-time handyman he utilized on occasion to speed up a job.

This job, he decided in a moment of raw honesty, needed speeding up. If only to get done faster because the sooner they were out of each others' lives the sooner things would go back to normal for him. Dull, but normal. Every treaty had an unpleasant part, he thought philosophically.

"Ginny acts like a kid in a candy store, waiting for me to come home," he told Ernie as they painted the renovated downstairs bathroom a shade of icy blue. "The minute I walk in through the door, she runs over to me and checks both my hands to see if I brought her anything."

Ernie dipped his roller into the tray, removing the excess paint before beginning to apply what was left on the roller onto the wall.

"And?"

"Usually, I have," Stone said with a somewhat helpless shrug.

Ernie paused, as if trying to get his facts straight. "So the woman whose house we're working on bakes for your daughter?" Ernie asked, momentarily taking a break—something he did with a fair amount of frequency.

Stone could hear the laugh in Ernie's voice. The handyman probably thought the woman slaved for hours making these edible "gifts" she was sending home with him. The way to a father's heart is through his kid, right?

"It's not like it's a hardship for her. The woman's a chef—"

"Wait, back up. You said her name was Danielle Everett?" he asked incredulously.

"Yes."

"You talking about *Danni* Everett?" Ernie asked, saying her name as it if was revered in his household. Or at least revered by him.

"Yes," Stone replied.

"As in *Danni's Desserts to Die For?*" he asked in disbelief. His voice quavered a little. "We're talking about the woman on the cable channel?" Ernie's voice rose a little higher with each sentence.

"Yes." Ernie was looking at him as if he were utterly starstruck. "I take it you've seen her show."

"Seen it?" Ernie repeated with a harsh laugh. "I never miss it. That woman cooks on all four burners and I'm not just talking about the stove." His laugh turned almost lusty. "*That's* who you're working for? Oh man, you lucky devil," Ernie crowed gleefully. "Anyone who looks like that has *got* to be able to really cook outside the kitchen, if you know what I mean." The man winked at Stone in an exaggerated fashion.

"My wife thinks I've developed an interest in her programs," he continued, chuckling. "I let her think whatever makes her happy." He scrubbed his hand over his face as he obviously envisioned the encounters between his one-time protégé and the woman who in his mind deserved a golden spatula. "So what's she like in person?" Ernie asked eagerly.

"She's nice." Stone thought that was a good, safe description, certainly not an offensive one and not one that could be regarded as giving away how he really felt about the woman.

"Nice?" Ernie echoed, then jeered. "Nice? An apple is 'nice,' a spring breeze is 'nice.' This woman is nothing short of hot. And if she's sending desserts home with you for your kid, that means she likes you," Ernie pointed out. "I mean *really* likes you."

Maybe he shouldn't have shared this, after all. He liked Ernie, but the man, now that he thought of it, wasn't exactly the last word when it came to being discreet. "I think you're reading too much into this, Ernie."

"And I think you're not reading enough into it," the handyman scoffed.

"Ernie, Danni and I have a professional relationship, that's all. I'm renovating her house and she's paying me to do it. End of story," he said firmly.

But Ernie remained unconvinced. He rolled his applicator down the wall one time, then paused again. "Huh. Nobody ever sent desserts home with me for my kid."

And there was a very good reason for that. "You don't have any kids, Ernie," Stone reminded him.

But Ernie was not about to be diverted from the stance he'd taken. "You're missing the point here, boy," he said impatiently.

There was no convincing the man tonight, Stone thought. The sooner he got him out of there, the sooner things would go back to normal—at least for the evening.

"And you're missing a spot," Stone said, pointing out a small section of the wall that Ernie's roller had skipped over. "Now stop making prophesies and finish that wall so we can get started on the upstairs bathrooms before she decides to hire another contractor."

"Will you introduce me?" Ernie asked.

"Sure, why not? I'll introduce you." Stone played his ace. "But only after you finish painting the bathroom."

"On it!" Ernie gleefully declared, putting some muscle into it.

Shaking his head, Stone got back to what he was doing.

Chapter Thirteen

Danni saw the truck from a distance as she turned down her block.

At first, she thought maybe it was just wishful thinking on her part, or she was seeing a truck that was actually sitting in the driveway next to hers.

But as she drew closer, she realized that it *was* her driveway. Stone's truck was still there, despite the fact that it was past six o'clock.

A smile curved her mouth as she pulled her car up next to the truck. Taping this week kept hitting snags and running way over the usual time, with her afternoons bleeding into her evenings.

Danni's sense of responsibility trumped her desire to get home early so that she could exchange a few words with Stone before he left for the day. She wanted to talk to him about how work was going, about how his daughter was doing.

About anything at all actually.

Lately, she found that she looked forward to seeing him. And never more than today.

Ever since he'd kissed her, she found that her mind kept straying at the most inopportune times to thoughts of Stone, to the way his laugh set off a reaction in the pit of her stomach.

The familiarity of that set off more chain reactions inside her.

So far, she and Stone, as well as his daughter, had spent several Saturdays visiting every conceivable store that carried tile, floor coverings and/or bathroom fixtures and accessories, within a forty-mile radius. She'd finally made all her selections, thanks to Stone's advice and guidance. But, he'd warned her, just because she'd placed the orders didn't mean that it was smooth sailing from then on. Not everything was arriving in a timely fashion as originally promised. There'd been delays and mishaps, and consequently, seven weeks into the remodeling she was still making do with a hot plate, a microwave and a plug-in grill.

When Stone apologized, she told him she knew it wasn't his fault and that she was getting used to "roughing it." The smile he gave her in return was well worth what she had to put up with.

If she didn't know any better, she would have said she was falling for the muscular contractor. But of course she knew better. Love took time. Time to cultivate, to develop. Stone had only been in her life for seven weeks.

That might be long enough for a fruit fly to fall in love, but not a woman, right?

Despite her sensible reasoning, Danni caught herself hurrying up the walkway to see Stone. However, she told herself it was for an entirely different reason than the fact that he made her pulse race.

Danni stopped at the door, forcing herself to take a deep breath. She needed to collect herself.

You're acting like a teenager hoping to ambush the school hunk, she chided herself. But the truth of it was, she had to admit, she *did* feel like a teenager. The idea of seeing Stone caused her pulse to pick up speed and anticipation to corkscrew all through her.

It had been a *long* time since she'd felt like this, she thought, opening her front door and walking in.

Even though she didn't see him, she could feel his presence—and right now, that was a very good thing.

She didn't want to be alone.

"Hello?" she called out.

"In here," the deep male voice called back. It was coming out of the kitchen.

Danni told herself not to pick up speed as she went through the house, but she did anyway. She stopped just short of the kitchen. Crossing the threshold, she made her way over to Stone. There he was carefully placing small tiles one at a time on the back wall, creating what would eventually be the backsplash over the new cook-top she'd selected last week.

"You're still here," she observed, pleased.

"Looks that way," he quipped. Then he glanced over his shoulder at her. "I felt bad about the kitchen still not being finished so I thought I'd stay longer to do some more work. I figured it was okay because you weren't home yet." Finished for now, he brushed his hands off on the back of his jeans. "But you're here now and you probably want the house to yourself, so I'll go."

She didn't want him to go, not yet. Rattling around the house tonight would feel exceptionally lonely to her. "Don't rush off on my account. I can always have the house to myself later," she told him. She needed to have a plausible reason to ask him to stay, otherwise, she would just seem needy to him. Danni fell back on a tried and true method. "Have you eaten yet?"

Stone nodded, thinking she meant had he eaten that day. "Had some kind of sandwich Virginia threw together for me for lunch—don't ask me what. I tend not to pay attention to things like that when I'm working."

That sounded like a typical male, Danni thought. Her father had been like that, eating without paying attention to what he was consuming.

"I can make some dinner for you," Danni offered, going into the family room where her old refrigerator was currently housed.

Stone knew better than to point out that she still had no stove. He'd watched her work miracles on her hot plate. She cooked better on the hot plate than most women did with a state-of-the-art stove.

Still, he didn't like putting her out on his account. "That's okay. Virginia probably has some takeout waiting for me."

The more the merrier, Danni thought. Especially tonight.

"Tell her to come by with Ginny," she said, impulsively extending an invitation to the rest of his family. "It's important for a little girl to eat dinner with her daddy."

Something in her voice caught his attention. A sadness he hadn't heard before. Granted he hadn't known her for that long, but he'd noticed that usually Danni was incredibly upbeat. And while there was a smile on her face right now, it appeared to be taking some effort on her part to maintain.

"Something wrong?" he asked her.

"No," she said quickly. "I just think that fathers and daughters should spend time together if they can." *When they can,* she added silently as another pang skewered through her.

"You'll get no argument from me, but Ginny's not neglected, if that's what you're thinking." And then he paused. Those were tears shimmering in her eyes even though she'd turned her head away quickly, he could swear to it. "There *is* something wrong, isn't there." It wasn't a question anymore. "Maybe it's none of my business," he acknowledged. "But I'm a pretty good listener if you want to talk."

She wanted to talk, but she didn't know if the words would even sound coherent when they came out. People endured loss all the time and went about their lives. For the most part, she'd gone on with hers, but there were just times, like now, when the loneliness threatened to undo her.

"I'd rather not be alone just yet, if you don't mind," she told him quietly.

That much he'd already gathered. "I'm not going any-where," he told her. Gesturing toward the open boxes of tile he had on the kitchen floor, he told her, "I've got enough tile there to work straight through the night." But right now, work—though he loved it—wasn't up-permost on his mind.

Stone crossed to her, studying Danni's face. "Some-thing did happen today," he guessed.

"No, not today. At least, not this year today." She blew out a breath. It was just as she'd thought, her words were getting jumbled. The man probably thought he was working for a lunatic. Maybe it was better if she ex-plained. "My dad died four years ago today," she said, her voice barely audible.

"I'm so sorry," he told her compassionately.

She sighed and a shaky breath escaped her lips. "Yeah, me, too."

"You were close, you and your dad?" Stone guessed.

She wanted to say yes, but that really wasn't true. At least, not for most of her childhood.

"Just at the end. He was a traveling salesman," she said with a half smile on her lips. "The kind they always tell stories about. He was on the road for most of my childhood. I grew up missing him. One of the last things he told me just before he died was how much he regret-ted not being there for me, not being there to share the simple things as well as the milestones. It wasn't until after he became ill that I found how smart he was and how funny. I felt cheated." She looked at him. "Don't let Ginny feel that way years from now."

He laughed softly and shook his head. "Not a

chance. She'd going to have the exact opposite to complain about—an old man who glares at her boyfriends
when they come to the door. Who keeps wanting to
hang out with her even though she wants to pretend he
doesn't exist because he's embarrassing her in front of
her friends." There was more truth than he was happy
about in his prophesy.

Danni smiled at him. He was instinctively a good father, she could just tell. "She might complain about it,
but deep down inside, she'll be grateful that you love
her enough to care."

"We'll see," he responded.

"I was serious about the invitation," she told him.
"About having Ginny and your sister over for dinner."

"Sounds good," he agreed. "But we can do it some
other night. I think that Virginia would appreciate a little
heads-up first. But I'll stay," he told her quickly in case
she thought he was trying to leave as well.

"I'm sorry. I'm acting like a child. You've put in a
long day, I shouldn't be making you stay longer."

"Well, I'm standing over here and you're standing
a couple of feet away from me and as far as I can see,
there's been no arm twisting going on so you're not *making* me do anything. Now, you can't issue an invitation
to dinner and then rescind it in the next breath. Not after
my salivary glands have started to drool in heated anticipation. You don't want to be labeled a culinary tease
now, do you?" He asked the question so seriously, for a
moment she didn't realize that he was kidding her.

"Heaven forbid." She laughed, appreciating his
kindness.

"Good, then go whip up dinner. Impress me with your ability to create something delicious out of nothing," he told her.

"I'll do my best." It felt good to laugh. Good to feel useful as well. A surge of deep gratitude spiked through her. "You're a good man, Stone Scarborough."

He shrugged off the compliment, not comfortable with its weight. "I'm only as good as I have to be," he told her.

Why that sounded like a promise of things to come to her she didn't know, but it did. And a little thrill of anticipation raced through her.

He was being awfully nice, which made her feel both vulnerable and guilty. Vulnerable because she was responding to this display of sensitivity on his part and guilty because she'd almost forced him to stay to keep her company. The man had a life waiting for him. Not to mention a girlfriend, the one that Ginny told her she didn't like.

"I'm sorry, I didn't mean to guilt you into staying. I'll be okay, really," she underscored. "You should go home to your daughter."

"So then you really are reneging on dinner?" he asked.

His expression seemed so serious, she didn't know if he was kidding or not. She told him the truth. "No, that's my way of telling you that you don't have to stay here and hold my hand."

"I know I don't *have* to stay," he replied. "Did it ever occur to you that maybe I was waiting for an invitation to stay?"

Danni shook her head, her eyes never leaving his. "No."

"No?" he questioned.

"No, it never occurred to me," she told him. She took another breath. She liked him and right now, he was keeping the shadows at bay for her, but she didn't want to be the cause of any discord in his life, no matter how innocent it actually was. "Stone, I have no right to ask you to stay for any reason other than work. You have a girlfriend—"

"Had," he corrected. Was that the problem? Talk about being selfless, she had to be at the head of the class. "I *had* a girlfriend."

He didn't ask Danni how she knew that he'd been seeing someone; he just assumed that any description of Elizabeth had to be something Ginny had told her. Most likely his daughter had complained about Elizabeth since she had never really warmed up to the woman— not that, looking back, he could blame her.

"You broke up?" she asked, stunned. Danni did her best to ignore the strong desire to cheer. "I'm so sorry." Danni tried to sound sincere, but it was hard sounding sincere when she felt like grinning.

"Don't be," Stone told her. "She gave me a choice, so I chose." It had been more of an ultimatum, and he didn't like ultimatums. He and Elizabeth weren't in a place in their relationship where that sort of thing mattered. "She didn't like the fact that I had canceled on her twice and she informed me that I had to choose between her and a job I was currently doing, so I chose the job. I don't like having my back against a wall," he told her simply. And then he shrugged again. "We weren't right for each other, anyway."

"I'm sorry to hear that," Danni said. But she really wasn't.

They talked all the way through dinner and Danni found herself laughing over his recollections of his first job in construction—when he had been less than able, just very willing.

For his part, Stone found her incredibly easy to talk to, which in his eyes was a big deal since he didn't readily share bits and pieces of himself with anyone.

That was how he found himself talking to her about Eva. About the four perfect years they had spent together and about how grief-stricken he was when the police came to his door late one afternoon to tell him that she'd been struck by a hit and run driver while she was out on her afternoon run. Eva was a physical fitness advocate who was always trying to get him to join her. He'd tried going out and running a few times before Ginny was born, but found he had no patience for it. He preferred lifting weights, so Eva ran alone.

Had he been with her that afternoon, he might have been able to push her out of the way, or gotten struck in her place.

For a very long time, he carried a great deal of guilt around with him. Guilt for being alive while Eva was dead.

"You can't do that to yourself," Danni told him, picking up his plate as well as her own and bringing them to the bathroom where the sink was still operational.

He followed behind her with the glasses and utensils. "Easier said than done," he pointed out.

Setting down the two plates in the bathroom sink, she turned in the doorway, about to get the rest of the dirty dishes.

She wound up brushing up against Stone. Startled, as lightning coursed through her at all the points of contact, she lost her train of thought for a second, then murmured, "Sorry."

He contradicted her by saying, "My fault."

Both apologies blended together and faded off into the netherworld. She offered him a small smile. "I've talked your ears off, I didn't mean to."

To which he went through the motions of touching his ears as if to see that they were still attached.

"Nope," he assured her, "they're still there. You didn't talk them off." And then he looked at her and smiled into her eyes. "Cut yourself some slack, Danni," he told her. "You've had a really rough time of it from what I've gathered."

She could feel the heat building up within her. Heat that the weather outside had nothing to do with.

"I could say the same thing to you," she told him, acutely aware of their close proximity, and how very easy it would be just to lean a little forward. Lean into him and from there, lean into a whole world of possibilities. Danni could feel her heart beginning to pound even harder than before.

"Would you mind if I kissed you?" he asked her, his voice lower than a whisper.

"No," she responded in the same sort of low voice

that Stone had just used. Danni could feel herself trembling inside.

Get a grip, Danni. Nothing's going to happen. Just stay firm and you'll be all right.

"I wouldn't mind," she told him.

He was asking for trouble and he knew it.

But her vulnerability spoke to him and the sadness in her eyes reached out to him, silently asking him for the only sort of comfort he could give her, comfort that transcended mere words.

Her breath caught in her throat as she felt him framing her face with his hands, felt his breath drifting along her face. Felt the almost fierce longing that had suddenly sprang up, fully formed, within her. Longing that reached out to him.

His lips came down on hers and this time, they both knew, there was no turning back.

Chapter Fourteen

Volleys of excitement shot through Danni.

It was too late to run for cover, too late to pretend that she didn't want this. She wanted it as much as she wanted to wake up tomorrow morning.

More.

Since her father had died, Danni had devoted herself exclusively to forging a future for herself, to making her cooking her own small cottage industry.

Other people with an aptitude for cooking or home-making had done it, putting their own spin on it, their own particular brand, and she felt that if she focused only on that, only on applying herself 24/7 to turning this goal into a reality, she stood a good chance of making it happen. That, in turn, would allow her to pay off the mountain of bills that all but haunted her.

She'd never thought she would take off the way she

had—which necessitated more energy, more focus and so much less "me" time for her.

Danni had almost forgotten that there was a "me" inside of her that required something other than working twenty-four hours a day. That knew how to do more than communicate with her audience, much as she cared about not disappointing them.

What she was feeling now, with Stone, opened a door for her to a place she'd ignored for so long, a place she hadn't even ever fully explored before.

A burst of sunshine went off inside of her as Stone's lips skimmed along the side of her neck, along the hollow of her throat. She could feel her insides quivering as anticipation began to swiftly build.

Without being aware of it, she dug her fingertips into the hard surface of his arms as she tried to anchor herself to him, to this wondrous sensation echoing through every fiber of her being. Glorying in it and wanting more, yet at the same time, being afraid of where this was taking her.

She felt disarmed, naked, vulnerable—and more alive than she'd been in far too long a time.

And then suddenly, as abruptly as it had begun, it stopped.

Stone stopped kissing her.

She felt him drawing away. Was something wrong? Had she done something to make him stop? Crossed some line she shouldn't have?

Confusion overtook her and she struggled to focus not just her eyes but her mind as well.

"Danni, are you sure?"

She saw his lips move, heard his voice echo in her head. The haze around her made it difficult for her to understand him at first.

It took her several moments to process the words. Several more to process the intent.

Dear God, was he being gallant? she wondered. She didn't know men like Stone existed outside of wishful thinking and maybe a few romantic comedies.

"And if I said no?" she asked, needing to hear what he would say.

Could he walk away from her, from this moment, just like that? Danni was fairly certain that she really couldn't walk at all right now. Her knees were weak and she'd all but turned into a swirling cauldron of pulsating needs. That made taking the smallest of steps all but impossible.

"If I asked you to, would you just back off?" she asked.

"Yes," he told her, his eyes caressing her even though his hands were still.

"Oh."

That meant he wasn't moved, didn't feel what she did. That he could take this or leave this at will. She could feel her heart sinking all the way down to her toes.

"It would kill me," Stone told her, "but I would." He framed her face again, his eyes intent on hers. "I won't lie. I really want you, Danni, but if you have the slightest bit of doubt, I'll stop. I don't want to force myself on you."

A laugh bubbled up in her throat. The rays of sunshine were back, stronger and brighter than they'd been before.

"What would you say to my forcing myself on you?" Danni whispered in his ear as the cauldron inside of her overflowed.

His mouth curved just a little, but she could feel the effects of his smile go all the way deep down into her soul.

"I'd say 'bring it,'" he told her.

And then there were no more words.

Words were next to impossible when he kissed her. Maybe she should have played harder to get, but the key word in that was *played* and she didn't want to play at this, didn't want to play any games at all. Games were for people who didn't feel what she was feeling. This sensation was far too serious for her to pretend otherwise, even if it meant saving face in the end.

She had no doubts that there would be regrets and possibly even soon. But Danni was certain that she'd regret not seizing this moment and making the most of it even more.

Heat soared through her as, wrapped in ardor, Stone and she moved from the barren kitchen with its patchwork of tile along one wall into the overly crowded family room with its makeshift, temporary obstacle course.

Danni was suddenly aware of the refrigerator directly at her back as Stone worked nothing short of magic with his lips along her torso, his fingers deftly removing more and more of her clothing as his clever mouth heated her skin.

Danni did her best to mimic his movements, letting

him take the lead only so that she could follow behind him almost immediately. Do what Stone did, create havoc within him the way he created it within her.

Her cool fingertips swept along his ribcage, pulling away the material that clung to his body by design as well as by his sweat.

Small, lethal tongues of fire licked at him as he felt her hands make short work of his T-shirt and his jeans, removing them almost as quickly as he was divesting her of hers.

And then, a short eternity later, there was nothing but skin between them. Stone trailed his hands along her body, memorizing curves and swells, committing every fraction of delicate inch to memory, lingering over every nuance he discovered.

Glorying in every involuntary sound conveying pleasure that she made.

Each time he heard one, he felt a corresponding surge of desire shoot through him, raising his need for the final moment. And yet, he wanted to keep it at bay for as long as he possibly could, wanting to revel in her, in holding her, in having her, for as long as he was able. Because, all things considered, there might not be another time and he needed to store up everything he was feeling against that eventuality.

The sofa, miraculously, didn't have a mountain of things piled onto its cushions. Somehow, it had escaped becoming a repository while everything else had been requisitioned to serve double duty when the kitchen appliances had moved in.

Consequently, that was where they ended up in their

blind dance of passion. On the sofa. Their bodies firmly molded against one another without an inch of space, or of sofa, to spare.

She found herself beneath him, with his weight just barely pressed against hers as he gathered her to him, covering every free inch of space on her body with his lips, his teeth, his tongue, effectively branding her from this day forward.

Danni tried to remain still, she really did, but she couldn't help herself. Twisting and turning, first into his kiss, then away as she savored what it was doing to her, was done almost involuntarily.

Done automatically.

Her body throbbing both in response to his actions and from a yet unfulfilled desire, Danni arched her back, pressing herself against him urgently. At the same time, she stroked any part of Stone she came in contact with, succeeding better than she'd possibly hoped when she heard him suddenly suck in his breath and he caught her hand.

She saw the look in his eyes and her heart all but stopped, then sped up again to the point that it felt as if it was challenging the speed of light.

Before she could say a word, she felt Stone parting her legs with his knee.

The next moment, they were joined together and another, far more intense, wave of heat flashed through her.

And then the race to the top, to the climax of their experience, began.

He set the tempo and she matched it, moving faster each time he did until finally, with his hands joined to hers just above her head, she felt the lightning explode and light the very sky in her world.

Felt the power seize and hold her before, all too soon, it began to recede.

Danni held on to it as long as possible, aware of just how tightly Stone was holding her to him, as if, were he able to, he would have absorbed her completely into himself.

A sense of loss nibbled away at the edges of her being when she felt the slight sag of his body against hers as Stone began the descent back down again.

Maybe it was selfish of her, but Danni wasn't quite ready to release the euphoria dancing through her. In a move more instinctive than anything else, she wrapped her legs around his torso, keeping him exactly where he was.

He raised himself up on his elbows and for a moment, just looked at her as he brushed the hair out of her face. She couldn't begin to gauge what he was thinking.

Stone smiled when he spoke. "Is that your way of saying you want more?"

"No," she answered, even though she *did* want more. "That's my way of saying I want to hold on to the sensation just a little bit longer."

About to roll off her and take his place right beside Danni, Stone remained where he was a while longer.

There were far worse places to be in the world, he thought with suppressed amusement. "Anything else?" he asked her.

She laughed then, a soft, gentle laugh that made him smile all the more. Things were going on inside of him that he didn't feel up to exploring. For now it was enough that there were these skyrocketing sensations going on in his body as a direct result of their close contact.

"You can relax," she told him. When he didn't move a muscle but continued looming over her, she added, "That means you can lie down next to me instead of staying where you are."

The next moment, he was rolling off her and gathering her to him. "Certainly didn't see that coming," he murmured under his breath.

"What?" She wasn't sure what he was referring to. "That I'd let you lie down?"

"No." He gently stroked her cheek, succeeding in arousing himself with the simple action. "That you'd let me—well, you know."

"There was no 'letting' going on," she assured him. "Whatever went on was done by mutual consent," she told him.

"Regrets?" he couldn't help asking her.

"Yes," she admitted. When she saw the sadness that entered his eyes, she was quick to add, "But not about this. Perhaps no one explained to you what the word *mutual* means?" she suggested.

He laughed and pulled her closer, then kissed the top of her forehead. "I know what it means. I suppose you'll want a friends-and-family discount on the work," he teased.

Danni raised herself up on one elbow, a part of her still rather stunned that she'd done what she had. Celibacy had become a way of life with her. "And just how does that work?" she teased back.

Stone did his best to keep a somber expression on his face as he said, "The closer a friend or a family member you are, the better the discount."

"I see." He was still flat on his back and she was looming over him on the limited space they were sharing. The ends of her hair were lightly flirting with his upper chest, tickling it. "And just how friendly am I allowed to get?"

"As friendly as you want," he told her solemnly—but his eyes were flirting with her the entire time.

"What if I want to be very, *very* friendly?" she pressed. "Then what?"

He pretended to think the matter over. And then he wove his fingers through her hair and said, "Then I just might wind up having to pay you for working on your house."

"Sounds tempting," she said, her eyes dancing as she regarded him.

"No, *you're* tempting," he corrected. Cupping the back of her head, he brought her face down closer to his. "So tempting that you'd probably be banned in at least seven Southern states," he theorized.

"How about you?" she asked. "Are you thinking about banning me?"

He slowly moved his head from side to side, his eyes never leaving hers. "My mother didn't raise any stupid children," he told her.

"Prove it," she whispered, her words feathering along his lips.

He laughed then, delighting in her, in the way she

made him feel. It had been a very long time since a woman had made him glad just to be alive.

"I thought you'd never ask," he told her, bringing her closer to him again.

It amazed Stone that he could want her again so soon, that he would be ready to make love with her all over again so quickly on the heels of what they had just done together.

He thought he knew his limitations, thought he knew himself as well as any man could know himself. But being with Danni had created a whole new set of parameters for him, parameters that both surprised him and pleased him at the same time.

He had no idea, at this moment, where any of this was going. All he knew right now was that he wanted her and that, for the first time in a very long time, he didn't feel as if there was a part of him that was empty, a part that was conspicuously missing. Maybe he wasn't exactly complete, but he wasn't empty, either.

And more than that, he realized as he began the journey back to paradise, he was happy.

Chapter Fifteen

"Happy" was a dangerous state to be in, Stone thought the next afternoon as he attempted to finish what he'd scheduled to be done for today.

He was hurrying. He wanted to be gone by the time Danni came home. The less temptation, the better.

"Happy" made you blind to the inevitable and set a man up to take a fall. And if ever a man was getting set up for a fall, it was him.

He *knew* there was no future for the two of them; he'd been here before. Granted, Danni was a far warmer person than Elizabeth had been, but they were both professional women, both smart and attractive—and Danni was a budding celebrity to boot. And he, he was a former aerospace engineer with a general contractor license who didn't talk all that much.

He just wasn't on the same level, the same rung in

society as Danni. Eventually that would hit her and become important enough to move to center stage even if it didn't seem that way now. He had nothing to offer her and he knew it. She outearned him and while that wasn't a problem for him, down the line it just might turn into one for her.

Elizabeth, he knew, was acutely aware of the fact that she earned more money than he did. She'd even mentioned it a couple of times in passing. The most notable time was when she'd talked about sending Ginny off to a "proper" private school, to use her words. She'd quickly followed that up by saying she knew he probably didn't have the money for that, given his job, but she did and she was quite willing to "lend" him the money so that Ginny could receive a decent education.

Though he'd tried to deny it to himself at first, it became very apparent that this was less about Ginny and more about her and how it would reflect on her to have a stepdaughter who went to public school.

After that incident, he was forced to acknowledge two things. One, Elizabeth apparently wanted to send his daughter away once they were married—something she'd obviously taken for granted despite his "station in life." And two, she did consider herself and what she did superior to what he did and consequently, to him.

After that, even if Danni hadn't come along, their relationship was scheduled for termination.

After measuring, he hung the last two tiles on the wall. He'd made a mistake last night. A glorious one, but a mistake nonetheless. To make certain that he wasn't tempted again—because the very thought of Danni sent him headlong into the land of heated desire—Stone decided that it was best not to be around her any more than was absolutely necessary. He only had so much willpower and no more.

Done! he congratulated himself as he rose to his feet.

Brushing off his hands, Stone looked around the immediate area to see what he needed to take with him. A quick assessment told him that he was going to need everything there tomorrow so there was no point in packing up.

Besides, it saved time.

Grabbing only the basic toolbox he brought with him to every job—a gift from Eva on their last Christmas together—he headed for the door.

As he put his hand on the doorknob, he felt it suddenly turning. The next second, the door was opening and Danni, her arms laden with bags and one large, opened box, came hurrying in.

The collision was inevitable. And jarring.

In that split second, Stone became acutely aware of her body and his own instant response to it. As if he needed to have that reinforced.

This would be a great deal more difficult than he'd foreseen, he thought with a suppressed sigh.

Steadying her even as he took a step back, Stone said, "You're home early."

Was that disappointment she heard in his voice, or just her imagination? Was she being insecure because she was still having trouble believing that something so perfect was happening to her at long last?

Damn it, Danni, you're overthinking things again. You plowed into him. He's just reacting to that.

"And you're leaving early," she noted, seeing the toolbox he'd dropped on the floor.

Suddenly feeling awkward, he said, "I got done ahead of schedule." It was only a partial lie; he'd gotten done early because he'd engineered it that way, but there was no way she could know about that. "So I thought I'd go home and spend some quality time with—um—with Ginny."

Great, forgetting your kid's name. If Danni needed any proof that you're less than brilliant, you just handed it to her.

If she noticed that he'd stumbled, she didn't show it. Instead, shifting the box and bags so she had a better grip, she told him, "Well, it looks like you can still get your wish."

Good, she wasn't going to try to make him stay, he thought. Maybe he'd overreacted as to the situation between them. Maybe she didn't feel the same way about him that he felt about her.

That was supposed to make him feel better, not worse, he upbraided himself. Just what the hell was the matter with him? Stone silently and impatiently demanded. Either he wanted her to be into him, or he didn't. He had to choose.

It was while he was confronted with this little dilemma that he realized she was all but completely overloaded with several bags and a large carton opened at the top.

And the most sensational aroma was wafting from it

all. "I'll just help you carry that in and then go," he said as he relieved her of the large opened box.

She looked up at him innocently. "I thought you said you wanted to spend some time with Ginny."

Confused, Stone followed her into the kitchen. The room now had a finished floor, so it could once more accommodate the table and chairs that had been there originally.

"I did—I mean—I do," he corrected.

"Then you'd better stay here because that's where they're coming," she told him matter-of-factly. Putting the bags down on the table she turned around to face him as she told him the rest of it. "I invited your sister and Ginny over for dinner."

"You're going to cook dinner now?" he asked, surprised.

She still didn't have a functioning stove, although that was next on his list of installations. Her new stove was currently in a box in her garage. He was waiting on the granite to be delivered for the counter. He knew, of course, the miracles she could accomplish with her hot plate, but that took time and it would be late before she would be finished.

"No, I'm going to *heat* dinner now, or at least keep it on a warming tray," she amended. "I made this at work before I left." She nodded toward the box and bags. "I'm kind of partial to the ovens we have on the set," she confessed. Which was why when she began ordering appliances to replace the ones she'd had before the remodeling began, she'd ordered the same brand of range and cooktop that was featured on her set. "This way Ginny and

Virginia won't have to sit around, starving and waiting for me to make a three-course meal one piece at a time on my struggling hot plate."

"When are they coming?" Stone asked.

He'd talked to Virginia earlier today and she hadn't mentioned anything about coming over for dinner. Why would she deliberately neglect to tell him that? Unless, it suddenly hit him, this was a last-minute idea on Danni's part.

The doorbell rang just then, interrupting his thoughts.

"Now," Danni said brightly, answering his question before she left the room.

She started to go to admit Virginia and Ginny. They were her buffer, because she really wanted to see Stone again, but at the same time, she didn't want either one of them to be tempted to repeat last night.

Not that she hadn't absolutely loved and thrilled at what happened between them. But an event of that magnitude stole away her ability to think clearly, causing her to focus on one thing and one thing only. And this was ever so much more complicated than "just one thing."

She didn't want him to feel pressured in the slightest while she needed to keep her intense, unvarnished reaction to him safely under wraps.

"You don't have to do this," he said just as she crossed the threshold.

She stopped and slowly turned around. Was he telling her, or actually ordering her not to do this?

"I know," she replied, flashing him a smile. "But I want to. From what you've told me, good, balanced meals aren't exactly a priority at your house."

With that, she hurried off before he could protest anymore. She didn't want to keep her two guests waiting any longer.

The second she opened the door, Ginny was quick to give her an energetic hug.

Virginia, on the other hand, hung back a little, which, Danni later discovered, that was rather foreign to her normal mode of behavior.

"You didn't have to invite me, too," Virginia told her. It was obvious that Danni had decided to make a play for her brother. Maybe she felt that the way to Stone was through his family.

Virginia smiled to herself. In that case, this woman was a very pleasant change from his last girlfriend. Elizabeth had made a point of looking down her perfectly shaped nose at her and the fact that she was self-employed, pulling in far less money than the other woman did.

But all this was supposition on her part and Virginia didn't want to seem as if she was presuming too much.

Danni laughed. "Well, it's certainly easy to see who you're related to. I'll tell you what I told your brother. 'I know I don't have to but I want to.' Come into the dining room while I still have a dining room where I can seat people," she said.

Taking Ginny's hand in hers, she led the way to the small room.

The only element that saved the dining room from arousing very real feelings of claustrophobia was that both sides of the room were open, leading into either the kitchen on one end or the living room on the other.

However the dining room itself was completely filled up by the scarred mahogany table with its six chairs. Of necessity, the table was placed at an angle so that people could pull out their chairs without slamming into walls on three of the table's four sides.

"Make yourselves comfortable," Danni told them. "Dinner will be ready in a few minutes."

Because she knew that form dictated it, Virginia felt she had to volunteer her services even though she was less than domestic.

"You need any help with dinner?" she asked Danni gamely.

Danni shook her head. "None whatsoever," she assured Virginia. "I prepared dinner at the studio. I just have to get all the covers off and make sure everything's the right temperature to serve," she told Stone's sister. "Besides, I wouldn't invite you to dinner and then put you to work cooking it. That wouldn't be right."

Virginia didn't bother hiding her relief. Turning toward her brother, she said, "I really like this woman, Stone," she said with sincerity as well as a bright, broad smile. Turning her head, she winked at her niece, who had been, after all, the start of it all when she'd brought her case to that Realtor. She'd had her doubts at first, but it looked now as if that woman was the genuine article. A matchmaker of the first caliber.

And neither one of these two people knew it, she realized. Somehow, that made this match all the more special.

"Me, too!" Ginny piped up, needlessly putting in her two cents.

No more than I do, Ginny, no more than I do, Stone said silently. Out loud he said to his daughter, "We already know that, kiddo."

If he didn't know better, he would have said that the female members of his family were actually trying to sell him on Danni.

As if they had to.

The real problem here was keeping his feelings under wraps—especially since he was so very tempted not to.

Had he been someone else, someone with fewer principles and more of an inclination to have a good time, he might have been tempted to go another route, to enjoy himself with Danni and live only within the moment without giving any thought to the future.

But that wasn't him.

He'd always done things with an eye to the future, ever mindful of the possible consequences of any action.

Stone already felt as if he cared more than he should for Danni. And he knew he was going to wind up paying for that. Because when the time came, and it would whenever he was finished with her renovations, they would inevitably go their separate ways.

He would move on to his next project and she would move on with the rest of her life. The life of a woman who had a bestselling cookbook to her name and a cable channel program that was swiftly growing in popularity. He'd heard somewhere that her audience was growing larger with each broadcast.

The last time he, Danni and Ginny had gone to look for new carpeting for her living room and bedrooms, the sales clerk had recognized her. And just like that, the man's clip, efficient manner transformed and he became a fawning fan who'd asked her for her autograph.

How could he possibly hope to compete with that? Stone wondered.

The simple truth of it was that he couldn't. He was destined to get lost somewhere in the background.

He was still mulling over this dark situation and its inevitable resolution when Danni returned with the main course and several side dishes. One that he was partial to, he noticed, while there were two others that would appeal to his daughter and his sister.

The woman thought of everything.

"Let me help," he offered, rising in his chair.

"You can help by eating," Danni told him, waving him back down with a plate of shredded hash browns covered in crushed cornflakes and mild, melted cheddar cheese. She placed the plate close to Ginny.

The asparagus, ham and cheese crepes found a home near Virginia while almond-sprinkled string beans were destined to keep Stone company.

The main course took the center of the table.

"Oh my God, what *is* this?" Virginia asked three minutes later as she took a second bite of the main course and rolled her eyes.

"Veal parmesan," Danni told her, carefully watching Virginia's reaction. It was hard to tell if that look was stunned appreciation—or aversion. "Why, is there something wrong with it?"

Danni had never made it a habit to taste her own food while she was preparing it, the way some other chefs did, so Virginia's question, voiced so quickly after she, Stone and Ginny had sat down to eat, made her a tad uneasy.

Still watching Virginia closely, Danni waited for more input.

"Wrong?" Virginia echoed incredulously. "Only in the sense that dying and going to heaven is wrong," she said with unabashed enthusiasm. "I've had veal parmesan once before, years ago, but I definitely would have remembered if it had tasted even a tiny bit as good as this does." She brought the next forkful to her mouth and it disappeared behind her lips. A contented sigh followed. "Definitely an out-of-this-world experience," she told Danni. "And you *made* this?" she asked, still unable to comprehend how a person could manage to make something so utterly spectacular.

"Yes," Danni replied with just the smallest touch of satisfaction and pride.

"Virginia," her brother said, a warning note suspended in the air.

"It's all right, Stone," Danni told him. "I really don't mind receiving positive comments. It's the negative ones that get to me."

"You get negative comments?" Virginia asked in utter disbelief.

"Sometimes," Danni answered.

Although, truthfully, she didn't remember the last time she had. Still, she wasn't one to take anything for granted and there had been a time when even though she'd always liked cooking, she hadn't been quite as good at it as she was now.

Stone listened in silence to the exchange between his

sister and the woman who made his body temperature rise just by smiling in his direction. The two, along with his daughter, seemed to be getting along rather well. From where he sat, the conversation seemed laid-back and completely unself-conscious, proceeding as if they had all known one other for years.

It filled him with a strange sort of melancholy, knowing that this was just temporary. That all too soon, this sort of contented air would all be in his past, a memory to be pulled out on occasion. When he finished the renovations to Danni's house, there'd be no more reason for them to see one another.

The renovations were what kept them together. It was the excuse he hid behind in order to see her.

Though it went against everything he believed in and practiced, Stone began to seriously entertain the idea of working just a little bit slower. Of getting less done each day, not more the way he'd initially planned.

It was the only way of hanging on to paradise a little longer. He knew he was just postponing the inevitable, but he didn't care. He was living within the moment and the moment contained Danni in it, which was all that really mattered to him.

Chapter Sixteen

It wasn't like him, but Stone found himself intentionally dragging his feet for as long as humanly possible.

He forced himself to work even slower after Ernie had called him. Prefacing his conversation by saying that he needed to pick up a little more extra work, Ernie asked him if he had anything available to throw his way. No job, Ernie told him, was too small. Then he'd asked him if work on "that cooking lady's house" was completed.

Ernie left him no choice.

It wasn't in Stone to lie, especially not to someone he knew and liked. So he'd said that he was still working on Danni Everett's house and that were a few things he could use a little help with completing.

Ernie was there the next morning, arriving before he did.

With Ernie working alongside of him, Stone did what

he could to stretch out the renovations on his end. He assuaged his conscience with the fact that Danni wasn't paying him by the hour, just by the project, so at least this wasn't costing her anything extra. And it was buying him some precious time.

But there was only so much he could do to stretch the process out without raising Ernie's suspicions and calling attention to the fact that he was moving like a man swimming in molasses.

The renovations, extensive as they were, were progressing smoothly with two pairs of hands working and completion was within sight.

Meanwhile, Stone's other campaign, the one whose theme was: look but don't touch, the one he'd come up with in hopes of keeping Danni at arm's length at all times, kept self-destructing at the starting line.

Most likely because his heart just wasn't in it.

Whenever they were alone together at the end of the day—after Ernie had left and Virginia and Ginny *weren't* coming over for dinner, all of Stone's attempts to strictly focus on his work just went flying out one of the newly installed double-paned windows.

Stone admittedly had gotten used to this, used to being with Danni, used to making love with her, to hearing the sound of her voice or catching a whiff of her perfume. In what amounted to an incredibly short amount of time, she had become part of his life.

Part of *him*.

Getting over Danielle Everett would be as hard as getting over an addiction.

Harder, because he couldn't hold an addiction in his arms the way he could hold her.

As if by mutual agreement, Stone noticed, they had both put off talking about it. Put off talking about life after the renovations were finally finished.

That's because there isn't going to be a life after the renovations are over, idiot, Stone upbraided himself. Danni was an intelligent woman. Which meant that she knew there was no future for them even better than he did. She was just too inherently polite to say as much out loud.

Maybe she even saw him as a guilty pleasure, he speculated. He certainly thought of her that way. Because she was. For him she was a very guilty pleasure and so much more.

No matter what he was doing, or what he was initially contemplating, thoughts of Danni would suddenly invade everything he did, everything he thought about.

With a flash of self-awareness, he came face-to-face with a truth that had somehow, without any warning, sneaked up on him.

He was in love with her.

Really in love with her.

"In love with a celebrity chef," he muttered under his breath, mocking himself as he laid there in her bed, watching her sleep.

They'd made love again at the end of the day, despite his very real determination—again—not to and afterward, she'd dozed off for a few moments.

"Hmm? Did you say something?" Danni asked, opening her eyes and looking at him.

Danni stretched languidly and he almost swallowed his tongue, becoming aroused all over again.

"What? No. I guess you must have dreamed it," he told her, the lie chaffing his conscience.

An embarrassed smile curved her mouth. "I must have dozed off," she realized aloud.

They'd made love, wonderful, exquisite love, and she'd been so very comfortable with him, she'd drifted off to sleep. It made her realize that he had become part of her life, a very integral part. How was she going to keep him that way?

"Can I make you something to eat before you go?" she asked, swinging her legs out of bed and then reaching down for her robe. The robe was usually at the foot of her bed, but it had managed to slide onto the floor, a casualty of their last lovemaking session.

"No," he murmured as he did his best to memorize her every movement. The way she stretched before she slipped the robe on, the way the silky material clung to her every curve. The way she breathed.

Everything.

Because it would have to last him a very long time.

Pulling her hair out from the back of her robe and letting it fall free, Danni turned around to look at the man who had so easily, so effortlessly infiltrated every corner of her life. "Are you all right? You sound a little strange." There was something different in his voice. She wondered if she should be worried.

The thought came out of nowhere.

Getting out of bed, in her estimation Stone pulled his clothes on like a man in a hurry.

"I'm finished," he told her, his voice still strained, distant.

"Finished dressing? Finished for the day? Or—finished with me?" she asked. There was something unsettling about his declaration and maybe she was being paranoid, but she needed him to clear it up.

To set her mind at ease.

He drew in a breath, as if to fortify himself, then said, "Finished with the renovations."

She pulled the robe tighter around her, suddenly feeling very cold despite the warm weather outside her bedroom window.

Was she being put on notice?

"There's nothing left to do?" she asked, feeling very nervous inside, like someone waiting for the bottom to drop out from beneath her feet.

He shrugged, trying to look casual about it even though there was nothing casual about the situation. "Just to collect payment on the final bill."

Was that it? Was that all what they had boiled down to? A final payment?

Money?

"And then what?" she heard someone with her voice ask.

Stone watched her for a sign, some indication that she wanted him to stay, to be something more than just this intense fling in her life.

He saw nothing.

Stone shrugged, feeling an emptiness already beginning to form in the pit of his stomach. "And then I guess I'll go on to another project."

"I see."

Not a word, not a single word from him about *them* as a couple. Nothing to indicate that any of this meant anything other than a hot time.

Suddenly unable to support her weight, Danni abruptly sat down on the edge of the bed.

There it went, she thought, the bottom. Dropping out from beneath her feet, sending her plummeting into an endless abyss.

"How much do I still owe you?" she asked, her voice echoing hollowly to her own ear.

The rest of your life. You owe me the rest of your life. Didn't you feel anything at all? How can you just sit there, sounding so controlled?

"I'll send you a bill," Stone said out loud.

"You do that," she told him. He was dressed and standing at her bedroom's threshold. *This is it, he's going. He's really leaving.* "Would you mind letting yourself out? I'm feeling a little tired."

Why wasn't she saying something? his mind shouted. *Because she's relieved, that's why,* a voice in his head mocked.

"No problem."

Yes, problem, Danni thought. *A huge problem. You just ripped out my heart and tap-danced all over it. Was this just another gig for you? Was that what I was to you, a 'project'? Nothing more than a pastime? While you were renovating my house, were you also renovating me just to satisfy your ego?*

She heard the front door closing downstairs. Hot tears stung her eyelashes.

The sound of the closing door was like a knife scraping across her heart, drawing blood. Danni shuddered as she began to cry in earnest.

Ginny came bouncing into the small bedroom Stone had converted into his office.

"Can I come with you when you go to work at Danni's house, Daddy? It's been a week and you haven't taken me." The little girl pouted as she looked at him.

He'd done his best to avoid talking about Danni and, up until now, Ginny hadn't asked anything. But he'd known it was just a matter of time before she did.

Time to clear this up and get it out of the way, he thought, resigned. "That's because I finished working on her house."

Ginny scrunched up her face. As if his words didn't compute. "You *finished* it? What does that mean?"

Ginny was far too gifted a child to not know what that meant, Stone thought, but he told her anyway. "That means that everything she asked me to do to the house is done and I won't be going over there anymore."

Ginny's smile drooped and she looked crushed. "But I thought you *liked* her."

This was just what he'd been afraid of. "That had nothing to do with it one way or another. Of course I liked her, Ginny. She was a nice lady."

"And that's all?" Ginny pressed, as if his words still weren't making any sense.

"What else is there?" her father asked, looking at her suspiciously.

Ginny seemed on the verge of blurting out something but instead shrugged and murmured, "Nothing, I guess."

Leaving the room, the disappointed little girl went out into her backyard. Planting herself on the swing her father had built for her, she began to think.

"Daddy!" Ginny called out, running to him as he let himself in the front door. It was the next day and she seemed impatient for him to come home. "Danni called and said you had to come right over."

Why wouldn't the woman call him on his cell, he wondered. "Why?" he asked suspiciously.

"She said her new shower was leaking all over the place and the water was raining in the kitchen."

He stared at his daughter for a moment, convinced she must have gotten the message garbled. "Water was 'raining' in the kitchen?" he repeated in confusion.

Ginny nodded her head vigorously. "From the shower, she said."

Stone thought a moment, trying to visualize what Ginny was telling him. "It's leaking through the floor?" he asked incredulously.

Ginny bobbed her head up and down again, no doubt grateful her father had filled in the blanks.

"Uh-huh. She said for you to come right away."

"Why didn't she call me on my cell?" he wondered again, this time asking the question out loud.

The small shoulders rose and fell in an exaggerated shrug. "I dunno. But she said to hurry."

"I'm going to call her—" he began, taking out his cell phone.

"She won't answer," Virginia said, coming into the room and to Ginny's rescue. The little girl had shared her impromptu idea with her. Virginia, impressed with the rather clever, if shaky, plan, decided there was nothing to lose by implementing it. "She said she was going to be too busy bailing. She said that you should just come right over."

"So you talked to her?" he asked, trying to get the story straight.

"After Ginny answered the phone, yes," Virginia confirmed. "Poor woman sounds frantic. Go rescue her," she ordered.

Stone sighed, shaking his head. He never took shortcuts with his work or with the materials he used. Something like this had never happened before, but he supposed there was always a first time.

"I'm on my way," Stone called out, hurrying out the front door.

Only after the door closed did Virginia and Ginny grin at one another as they high-fived.

That's odd.

Mystified, Danni placed the phone back in its cradle. Ginny had just hung up after telling her that her father had instructed her to call and say he was coming to check out the upstairs-bathroom plumbing.

Ginny hadn't been very clear, saying it was something about a leak, but that she wasn't very sure because her father was hurrying out the door when he asked her to call for him.

Danni supposed it was all part of the contract and

his standing behind his work. If only he was that conscientious about standing behind his silent promises...

*Stop it. He left you. His choice, not yours. You're not
to look needy around him, understand?*

Danni told herself to remain aloof when he came over.
But in her heart she knew it was going to be damn hard
not to just throw herself at him.

Maybe this was just an excuse on his part to come
see her. Maybe—

If it was an excuse, then he'd act on it and she'd know.
No point in getting ahead of things and letting her imagination run away with her.

God, but she had missed him, Danni couldn't help
thinking as she checked her makeup in the mirror—a
mirror he'd picked out for her. One week and it felt like
one eternity.

"That's it, Danni, play hard to get," she upbraided herself, annoyed at her lack of resistance to the very idea
of Stone. "He walked away from you, you didn't push
him out the door, remember?"

The pep talk wasn't working.

She almost jumped out of her skin when the doorbell rang a few minutes later. It took everything she had
not to just fly to the front door to answer it. But she did
hurry, stopping just at the door.

Taking a deep breath, she opened it. When she did,
when she admitted him and looked up at Stone, her heart
hurt.

"Hello," she said formally. Stiffly.

Oh God, maybe he should have sent Ernie in his
place. The handyman was equal to anything and he

would have paid Ernie well to stand in for him. To take this bullet to the chest for him.

Stone walked in and she closed the door behind him. "Well, I'm here."

Danni stepped away from the door and in front of him again. Was he playing some game? Why? Did he want to see how unhappy his walking out had left her? "I can see that."

He couldn't continue addressing his words to the air. Bracing himself, Stone turned around to face her. "So, where's the emergency?"

She looked at him, confused. "Excuse me?"

"The leak," he emphasized. "Where is it?"

Why was he almost shouting at her? "I don't know, you tell me. You're the one who wants to check it out."

Was this some kind of game? Why was she playing dumb like this, as if she didn't know why he was here? "Because you called about it."

Now Stone was just plain making things up. "No, I didn't."

Her indignation seemed sincere. Stone regarded her closely. "Ginny told me you called and said the upstairs shower was leaking."

What was he talking about? "Ginny called to tell me you were coming to check out the pipes," she countered.

Something didn't smell right to him. He needed to get to the bottom of all this. "That doesn't make any sense, why would I want to check out your pipes—"

"Maybe you *like* them," she shouted at him, her nerves utterly frayed.

Stone could only stare at her. "What?"

Danni threw up her hands. "Never mind, I'm babbling." And then, abruptly, it hit her. "We've been set up. Think about it," she stressed, waiting for the light to dawn on him.

It did—even though it seemed impossible. "By a four-year-old?" he asked in disbelief.

"A very intelligent four-year-old. 'Four going on forty.' Those were your words, remember?" Danni pointed out.

"Yeah, I do." He looked at her for a long moment. It seemed almost inconceivable to him to have missed someone as much as he had missed Danni—but he had. With every fiber of his being. "Maybe she saw something we didn't."

Danni's eyes met his. "Or saw something we did, but refused to acknowledge."

Stone was about to tell her that she wasn't making any sense—except that she was. What hadn't made any sense, he realized, was his accepting defeat before a single shot had been fired. That wasn't like him. Because Eva's death had devastated him the way it had, it made him afraid of reaching out for what was right in front of him. That was no way to live. That wasn't life, that was as good as being dead and he wasn't going to accept it anymore. "Yeah, maybe that's it." He took a breath. "Danni, will you marry me?"

Her mouth dropped open. They had just gone from *A* to *Z* without stopping at any of the other letters. "What?"

"Will you marry me?" he repeated more forcefully. "I don't care that you earn more money than I do, I don't care that you're famous and I'm not—and I'm betting that you don't care, either. I did you a huge disservice before, thinking those things mattered to you, that because I was a contractor, you'd think I had nothing to offer you, but I do. I have my heart to offer you, freely and unconditionally and nobody's going to make you a better offer than that or ever love you more than I do." He had all but run out of breath, getting all that out before Danni could interrupt him. "So, again, will you marry me?"

Stunned, Danni could only stare at him in silence.

The silence stretched out between them, growing longer. And more silent. Until it became unbearable for Stone to endure a moment longer.

He'd finally said it, finally put himself on the line. He'd given her the gist of why he'd left and told her how he felt about her. Told her that he wanted her to marry him.

But she wasn't saying anything.

Why wasn't she saying anything?

Had he presumed too much after all? Stone wondered nervously.

Wasn't she *ever* going to say anything?

"Danni, I'm standing here, naked, out on a limb," he told her impatiently. "Aren't you going to say *anything* to me?"

"Wait," Danni ordered, putting up a hand for him to hold his tongue. "I'm savoring the image of you standing there, naked." Unable to maintain a straight face any longer, she burst out laughing. She felt like hugging the immediate world. "What do you want me to say?"

He was through beating around the bush. "'Yes' would be nice."

She smiled again, a softer killer of a smile. "Yes would be very nice," she agreed. Threading her arms around Stone's neck, she looked up into his eyes and said, "So yes. I say yes. Yes, I will marry you. Yes!" Her voice grew louder in volume each time she said the all important word.

Laughing, he pulled her closer to him. "And now you can stop saying it." And just to insure that she understood, he sealed his lips to hers.

Danni stopped saying yes verbally, but she continued saying it in other ways—just so that there would be no misunderstanding.

* * * * *

Don't miss Marie Ferrarella's next romance,
THE COLTON RANSOM, available July 2013
from Harlequin Romantic Suspense!

When a dangerous storm hits Rust Creek Falls, Montana, local rancher Collin Traub rides to the rescue of stranded schoolteacher Willa Christensen. One night might just change their entire lives....

***

"Hey." It was his turn to bump her shoulder with his. "What are friends for?"

She looked up and into his eyes, all earnest and hopeful suddenly. "We are, aren't we? Friends, I mean."

He wanted to kiss her. But he knew that would be a very bad idea. "You want to be my friend, Willa?" His voice sounded a little rough, a little too hungry.

But she didn't look away. "I do, yes. Very much."

That pinch in his chest got even tighter. It was a good feeling, really. In a scary sort of way. "Well, all right, then. Friends." He offered his hand. It seemed the thing to do.

Her lower lip quivered a little as she took it. Her palm was smooth and cool in his. He never wanted to let go. "You better watch it," she warned. "I'll start thinking that you're a really nice guy."

"I'm not." He kept catching himself staring at that mouth of hers. It looked so soft. Wide. Full. He said, "I'm wild and undisciplined. I have an attitude and I'll never settle down. Ask anyone. Ask my own mother. She'll give you an earful."

"Are you trying to scare me, Collin Traub? Because it's not working."

He took his hand back. Safer that way. "Never say I didn't warn you."

She gave him a look from the corner of her eye. "I'm onto you. You're a good guy."

"See? Now I've got you fooled."

"No, you don't. And I'm glad that we're friends. Just be straight with me and we'll get along fine."

"I am being straight." Well, more or less. He didn't really want to be her friend. Or at least, not *only* her friend. But sometimes a man never got what he wanted. He understood that, always had.

Sweet Willa Christensen was not for the likes of him....

***

Enjoy a sneak peek at **USA TODAY** *bestselling author Christine Rimmer's new Harlequin® Special Edition® story,* **MAROONED WITH THE MAVERICK,** *the first book in* **MONTANA MAVERICKS: RUST CREEK COWBOYS,** *a brand-new six-book continuity launching in July 2013!*

REQUEST YOUR FREE BOOKS!

2 FREE NOVELS PLUS 2 FREE GIFTS!

⬦ HARLEQUIN®

SPECIAL EDITION

Life, Love & Family

SADDLE UP AND READ 'EM!

This summer, get your fix of Western reads and pick up a cowboy from the HOME & FAMILY category in July!